A City Girl

by

John Law

(Margaret Harkness)

edited with an introduction and notes
by Deborah Mutch

Victorian Secrets 2015

Published by

Victorian Secrets Limited
32 Hanover Terrace
Brighton BN2 9SN

www.victoriansecrets.co.uk

A City Girl by John Law (Margaret Harkness)
First published in 1887
This Victorian Secrets edition 2015

Introduction and notes © 2015 by Deborah Mutch
This edition © 2015 by Victorian Secrets
Composition and design by Catherine Pope

Cover image shows Eliza Edwards, great-grandmother of Deborah Mutch.

A catalogue record for this book is available from the British Library.

ISBN 978-1-906469-54-2

CONTENTS

INTRODUCTION

'A Passive Mass': A Defence of *A City Girl*

Warning: This introduction contains plot spoilers

Margaret Harkness's first novel, originally published by Henry Vizetelly in 1887 under her pseudonym 'John Law', is the story of Nelly Ambrose, a beautiful working-class seamstress, and the consequences of her affair with handsome middle-class Arthur Grant. The novel, however, is best remembered not for its plot but as the trigger for Friedrich Engels's definition of realism in his thank-you note[1] to the author for his copy. Harkness was to become close to Engels, forming a friendship with Eleanor Marx and joining what the Social Democratic Federation's (SDF) periodical, *Justice*, termed the 'Marxist clique.'[2] It was Harkness who first conducted Eleanor Marx around the slums of London's East End, took Olive Schreiner under her wing during her early years in London and introduced her second cousin, Beatrice Potter, to Marx, Schreiner and Amy Levy[3] as well as to her future husband, Sidney Webb. Engels's friendly letter expressed his enjoyment of reading the novel, set out his ideas on the genre of realism and partly defined realism as a form which 'to my mind, implies, besides truth of detail, the truthful reproduction of typical characters under typical circumstances'.

British socialism was a highly literary movement and the close relationship between socialist politics, polemic and literary production is the focus for

---

1 The full transcript of Engels's letter can be found in Appendix A.
2 Anon., 'The Marxist Clique', *Justice*, 28 February 1891, p.1. The brief, unsigned paragraph (probably by either the chairman of the SDF Henry Hyndman or *Justice* editor Harry Quelch) on the editorial front page complained of the 'baneful' personal influence of Friedrich Engels on British socialism as 'the head of that Marxist clique' and his 'intrigue against and vilif[ication of] any Social Democratic organisation which is not under its direct control'. The full list of the clique was given as: 'Friedrich Engels, H. H. Champion, Edward Aveling, Eleanor Marx, Maltman Barry, John Burns, Tom Mann, Keir Hardie, W. Parnell, Margaret Harkness ("John Law"); with them has been closely associated, though happily he is opposed to their methods in some particulars, Cunninghame Graham.'
3 Deborah Epstein Nord, *Walking the Victorian Streets: Women, Representation and the City* (Ithaca, NY: Cornell University Press, 1995), p.185.

this introduction. Raphael Samuel noted a strong artistic impulse in the *fin-de-siècle* British socialist movement: from Tom Mann's formation of a Shakespeare Mutual Improvement Society, through Ramsay MacDonald's poetic oration at Keir Hardie's funeral, to Ethel Snowden's statement on the necessity of culture to society.[4] The socialist movement produced and attracted authors whose work has transcended the period (William Morris, H. G. Wells and George Bernard Shaw, for example) and those who, despite not having the same longevity, were phenomenally popular at the time (authors such as Charles Allen Clarke, Robert Blatchford and A. Neil Lyons). Margaret Harkness's slum novels (*A City Girl*, 1887; *Out of Work*, 1888; *Captain Lobe*, 1889; *A Manchester Shirtmaker*, 1890; and 'Connie', 1893-94) were very much a part of the socialist literary narrative and this introduction will discuss the novel as both a literary and a socialist text.

Realism, Socialism and the Political Context

Harkness's experience in the slums – and particularly the time spent at the East End Dwellings Company philanthropic project at Katherine Buildings, Whitechapel – provided her with detailed insight into the everyday lives of the poor: her typical characters under typical circumstances. She had accompanied Beatrice to Katherine Buildings while Potter was working as a rent collector for some months in 1885 and 1886. The women alternated their living accommodation between Potter's family home at Cheyne Walk, Chelsea, and rooms at Katherine Buildings, so Harkness describes the fictionalized version – Charlotte's Buildings in the novel – with what appears to be photographic accuracy and unflinching, unsentimental detail:

> The Buildings were not beautiful to look upon; they might even have been termed ugly. Their long yellow walls were lined with small windows; upon the rails of their stiff iron balconies hung shirts, blankets and other articles fresh from the wash-tub. Inside their walls brown doors opened into dark stone passages; and narrow winding staircases led from passage to passage up to the roof. (43)

The unlovely buildings are set in a similarly unlovely location: one side of the Buildings look onto the Royal Mint with its '[f]our tall chimneys and huge reservoir' (43), the children of the buildings attend school 'on the other side of the railway-bridge which faces Wright Street' (44) and out

---

4   Raphael Samuel, 'Theatre and socialism in Britain (1880-1935)', in *Theatres of the Left 1880-1935: Workers' Theatre Movements in Britain and America*, ed. by Raphael Samuel, Ewan MacColl and Stuart Cosgrove (London: Routledge & Kegan Paul, 1985), pp.3-73.

of school the children play 'on a plot of ground in which bricks and stones lay about' (51). This detailed positioning of the Buildings reinforces the sense of realism as, from this description of the immediate area (and others throughout the novel), a reader can easily locate the geographical spaces the characters inhabit. As a result of slum clearances, Second World War bombs and urban renewal, Wright Street has been obliterated, Katherine Buildings has also gone and the Royal Mint has relocated. Despite this, the reader can still trace the characters' movements thanks to Harkness's detailed description of the urban surroundings, much of which remains relatively unchanged. This association of the story with locatable spaces outside of the novel encourages the reader to accept the 'reality' of the story but is there such a thing as 'photographic accuracy' or 'photographic realism' in fiction?

Recent work on realism and photography has argued that photography was as much a work of fiction as literature which, rather than expand and individualize the pictorial representation of human beings, created a taxonomy where images 'acquired their meaning, not in relation to the body and by virtue of their resemblance to actual persons, places and things, but strictly within a system of images and by virtue of their difference from all other images in that system'.[5] This drive to categorize, according to Nancy Armstrong, is a desire to find or impose a stable unity on the world in order to know and contain reality but the categories, being themselves fictions, in effect limit the knowledge of the 'whole'.

It might be argued that Harkness is resisting this taxonomical impulse by presenting her written version of reality through the wider and unflinching gaze desired by theorists of realism from George Eliot to Georg Lukács. In 'Natural History of German Life: Riehl', Eliot criticized the artistic impulse to idealize the workers – in art, literature and on the stage – and sought a 'real knowledge of the People, with a thorough study of their habits, their ideas, their motives',[6] while Lukács praised the novels of Willi Bredel for presenting 'a picture that is correctly conceived from the standpoint of its content' but lamented the absence of 'living human beings, with living, changing and developing relationships between them'.[7] Harkness's unsentimental

---

5   Nancy Armstrong, *Fiction in the Age of Photography: The Legacy of British Realism* (Cambridge, MA: Harvard University Press, 1999), p.22.

6   George Eliot, 'Natural History of German Life: Riehl' (1856), in *Prose by Victorian Women, An Anthology*, ed. by Andrea Broomfield and Sally Mitchell (New York: Routledge, 1996), pp.173-206 (p.178).

7   Georg Lukács, 'The Novels of Willi Bredel', in *Georg Lukács Essays on Realism*, ed. by Rodney Livingstone (London: Lawrence and Wishart, 1971), pp.23-32 (pp.24-25).

presentation of location is married with a similarly clear-eyed and rounded image of the workers themselves: protagonist Nelly's beauty is set alongside the violence of her brother Tom, the kindness and generosity of the old soldier and his wife has its obverse side in their drunken domestic violence, the communal support for Susan's pilgrimage to Lourdes as she sets off 'with five shillings from the casuals in her pocket' (85) is contrasted with the regular violence George the caretaker must control: '[l]ast night he had fetched in the police to stop two women fighting; he had been called up to the top balcony where a man was kicking his wife, and no sooner had he come down than he had found a man stabbing a pal with a knife' (55). Thus the reader is introduced to a community of people who are neither entirely decent nor entirely unregenerate.

Nevertheless, Eileen Sypher has criticized Harkness's fiction for creating new 'types' of character in her novels, arguing that although 'her novels try to dismantle conventional stereotypes of the working class, they perpetuate others' such as 'the dock worker, the East End mother, the labor mistress'.[8] While there are reductive stereotypes in *A City Girl* – Nelly's thuggish brother and the vicious sweater's wife, for instance – Nelly's personality, individuality and strength of character develop as she matures from the vain, dreaming 'masher'[9] to the grieving mother and Arthur Grant's protector by her refusal to name him as her child's father. Similarly, Nelly's working-class suitor, caretaker George, is not reduced to the type 'lover': his small and large 'c' conservatism gives him a pragmatism that grounds him in the capitalist ideology imposed on the workers as he refuses to marry Nelly before he had 'bettered' himself. Although he is the saviour of Nelly after her expulsion from the family home, this is again presented through the pragmatic act of taking her to the Salvation Army rescue home, rather than any idealist notion of marriage and therefore legitimacy for the unborn child.

Despite this apparently realistic presentation of working-class life in London and after his initial praise, Engels continues:

> Now your characters are typical enough, as far as they go; but perhaps the circumstances which surround them and make them act, are not perhaps equally so. In the 'City Girl' the working class figures are a passive mass, unable to help itself and not even showing (making) any attempt at striving to help itself. All attempts to drag it out of its torpid misery come from without, from above. Now if this was a correct description about 1800 or 1810, in the days of Saint-Simon and Robert Owen, it cannot appear so in

---

8   Eileen Sypher, 'The Novels of Margaret Harkness', *Turn-of-the-Century Women*, 1.2 (1984), 12-26 (p.23).

9   *Masher*: See Chapter I, note 10.

1887 to a man who for nearly fifty years has had the honour of sharing in most of the fights of the militant proletariat.

It is true that there is no suggestion of socialism in either the foreground or the background of the story and, considering the activities of the socialist groups and the author's association with the Social Democratic Federation (SDF) during this period, it is certainly cause for comment. In September 1885, 30,000 to 50,000 radicals joined with socialists from the SDF, William Morris's Socialist League and the Fabian Society and took to the streets to protest against the closure of a site for open-air meetings in Dod Street, Limehouse;[10] the West End Riots of 8 February 1886 (alternatively referred to as Black Monday), the result of a counter demonstration organized by the SDF against a Free Trade meeting at Trafalgar Square, had caused panic among the middle and upper classes, and resulted in the leading SDF members Henry Mayers Hyndman, Henry Hyde Champion, John Burns and Jack Williams being tried and acquitted of inciting riot;[11] there were 48 branches of the SDF reported at the annual conference in 1887; its periodical, *Justice*, was selling enough copies to cover the publication costs;[12] and in November 1887, a matter of months after the publication of *A City Girl*, a series of demonstrations in Trafalgar Square against homelessness, unemployment and free speech culminated in the fatalities of 13 November – termed 'Bloody Sunday' – and the arrests of Fabian Annie Besant, SDF member John Burns, and the independent M.P. Robert Cunninghame Graham.[13] Given this political background, it is little wonder that Engels baulked at the presentation of a non-socialist, politically apathetic social group. For Engels, an apolitical description could not be a realistic presentation of working-class life in 1887.

Lynne Hapgood reads Harkness's male protagonist, Jos Coney, in her second novel *Out of Work* (1888), as existing in 'a state of political impotence',[14] which reflects Harkness's own political impotency as an unenfranchised woman. In *A City Girl*, Nelly is not only politically impotent

---

10 E. P. Thompson, *William Morris, Romantic to Revolutionary* (Pontypool: Merlin, 2011), pp.394-399.

11 Paul Addleman, *The Rise of the Labour Party, 1880-1945* (Abingdon: Routledge, 2014), p.5.

12 Martin Crick, *The History of the Social Democratic Federation* (Keele: Keele University Press, 1994), p.47.

13 E. J. Hobsbawm, *Labour's Turning Point 1880-1900*, (Brighton: Harvester Press, 1983), p.25; E. P. Thompson, p.575.

14 Lynne Hapgood, 'The Novel and Political Agency: Socialism and the Work of Margaret Harkness, Constance Howell and Clementina Black', *Literature and History*, 5.2 (1996), 37-52 (p.46).

but also ignorant as she responds to Arthur Grant's query about her interest in politics with a blush and the statement that 'she knew nothing about politics' (61). The women of the novel are generally presented as absent or excluded from political discussion: in Charlotte's Buildings 'the mothers gossiped in the doorways, the men smoked and talked politics on the balconies' (43) and Arthur does not attempt to address Nelly's political ignorance by engaging her in discussion. Instead he turns his attention to his male companions and 'began to discuss the Irish question with Jack, who was keen on the subject, and with George, who, however, said very little, and looked rather bad tempered' (61). Consequently the exclusion of women from politics, and through that the denial of agency and power, leaves Nelly (and women generally) on the outside of the conversation and with very little control over their own lives. Nevertheless, unlike Hapgood's reading of Jos Coney, the male characters of *A City Girl* – the middle-class Arthur Grant, the working-class George and his friend Jack – are all, in different ways, politically interested or active. Arthur Grant, as a wealthy middle-class man, was given his vote in the 1832 Reform Act and the working-class men would have obtained their vote under the 1867 and 1884 extensions of the franchise. However, as Engels notes, there is no suggestion that any of the characters' political agency would be wielded on behalf of socialism. As a middle-class man it is not surprising that Grant supports the Radical branch of the Liberal Party, but Jack is an active member of the Radical Club and introduces both George and Nelly to Arthur Grant. The only character who is shown as having exercised his right to vote is George and his choice is based on class deference: he voted for the Conservative Party because 'the Conservatives had the most money, so it was best not to offend them' (55).

So does the omission of socialist politics make Harkness a poor realist? In her response to Engels's letter[15] she capitulates to his criticism, accepting 'the want of realism' in her novel and blaming both her 'want of confidence in [her] powers' and her sex. Subsequent critics have joined Harkness and Engels in their censure of her realism in *A City Girl*, often preferring to discuss her second novel, *Out of Work*, as a better example of her realist fiction. Ingrid von Rosenberg laments Harkness's failure to learn from Engels's advice and carrying on 'drawing her grim pictures of the downtrodden';[16] Eileen Sypher condemns Harkness's fiction as a 'transparent' presentation of 'a conservative,

---

15   See Appendix B.
16   Ingrid von Rosenberg, 'French Naturalism and the English socialist novel: Margaret Harkness and William Edwards Tirebuck', in *The Rise of Socialist Fiction, 1880-1914*, ed. by H. Gustav Klaus (Brighton: Harvester Press, 1987), pp.151-171 (p.160).

patronizing, paternalistic perspective on both the working class and women's independence' written by an author who is 'intimidated by the middle-class textual reader';[17] Kevin Swafford accepts Engels's reading that 'by exclusively illustrating the passivity of the East End working class, Harkness fails to adequately represent the corresponding relationship between the historical reality of the London slums and the political behaviors of the urban poor and working class – thus her realism is faulty';[18] and Elizabeth Carolyn Miller similarly sides with Engels: 'The book is subtitled "A Realistic Story," but it simply does not ring true with his experience among the proletariat'.[19] But would a woman with a 'want of confidence' feel herself able to challenge the literary criticism of the international leader of the proletariat? Or might her capitulation be tongue-in-cheek? This is the woman, after all, who introduced Eleanor Marx to the slums and who, unlike the wealthy Engels, had lived among those she described. A closer look at the temporal as well as material setting might problematize these accusations of working-class passivity levelled at the novel.

Engels's assumption was that the work was set in the present-day ('it cannot appear so in 1887') and there are a number of indicators within the fiction that suggest this was the case. The chronology for *A City Girl* is not as clearly defined as *Out of Work*, which opens with Queen Victoria's jubilee procession through Whitechapel in June 1887 and includes a fictionalized account of the Bloody Sunday demonstration in Trafalgar Square in November of the same year. Nevertheless, the Albert Palace, where Nelly spends a happy day with George, Jack and Arthur Grant, was opened in 1885 and closed in 1888, reinforcing the assumption of a generally contemporary setting. Similarly, the real-life counterpart to Charlotte's Buildings began housing tenants in 1885. Despite this clearly signposted relationship between the content of the fiction and the material and temporal landscape outside of the novel at publication, the dating of Charlotte's Buildings begins to disrupt this certainty. The narrator states that 'the buildings were, at that time, about two years old' (42) which, if Charlotte's Buildings mirrors the history of its counterpart Katherine Buildings, would date the story in the year of its publication: 1887. But that brief aside – 'at that time' – is troublesome: the novel was published

17 Eileen Sypher, *Wisps of Violence, Producing Public and Private Politics in the Turn-of-the-Century British Novel* (London: Verso, 1993), p.109.
18 Kevin Swafford, *Class in Late-Victorian Britain, The Narrative Concern with Social Hierarchy and its Representation* (Youngstown, NY: Cambria Press, 2007), pp.44-45.
19 Elizabeth Carolyn Miller, *Slow Print, Literary Radicalism and Late Victorian Print Culture* (Stanford, CA: Stanford University Press, 2013), p.97.

in early 1887 when the age of the Buildings *was* two years, so what 'time' is the narrator occupying? The phrase suggests a retrospective narrative at odds with the dating of the material landscape and a fictional future with a generally passive working class would indeed be depressing to a revolutionary socialist such as Engels.

However, a near-past political setting, as suggested by Arthur Grant's lecture at the Radical Club, complicates the near-future narrative position:

> First he spoke of Radicalism upon the Continent; the expulsion of the Princes in France, and the increasing number of Socialists in Germany. Afterwards he drew the attention of his audience to the division in the Liberal camp; and said, as the Liberals were so divided, he hoped that the Conservatives would come into office, and give the Radicals time to organise themselves into a strong political party. (55)

Grant's wish for a Conservative government to allow the Radicals to regroup suggests that his speech is delivered during the Liberal Party's period of turmoil over Ireland and Home Rule. The collapse of the Liberal government in June 1885 brought in a Conservative caretaker government between June and January 1886. The general election held over November and December 1885 returned a Liberal minority government with Charles Stewart Parnell's Irish Nationalists holding the balance of power. The Parnellites were persuaded to support the Liberal Party with Gladstone's promise of an Irish Home Rule Bill, but the Bill was opposed from within the party by Liberal Unionists, including Joseph Chamberlain and Lord Hartington. The defeat of the Bill caused the collapse of this minority government and triggered another General Election in July 1886. This time a Conservative government bolstered by Liberal Unionists was returned and remained in power from July 1886 until August 1892. The turbulence and division within the Liberal Party is noted even before Grant delivers his speech as the narrator differentiates between Unionists and those open to the arguments for Home Rule: 'The Radicals call the Liberals milk-and-water Hartingtons, the Liberals call the Radicals crack-brained Gladstones' (54). Although the division between Radicals, Liberals and Unionists was not limited to the mid 1880s the political period is narrowed by the actions of George who 'had just given his vote to a Conservative candidate who had canvassed the buildings' (54). Thus, Grant's hope and George's vote set the story in a fictional world where an election is taking place.

An author as involved in socialist politics as Harkness was at this point would not be confused as to whether or not there was a General Election happening in the year she set her fiction. Nor, it would appear from the allusions to recent political debates and history, would her intended reader: the process of annotating *A City Girl* has made clear the political and social knowledge that was assumed to be held by the implied reader. Therefore it is in the close reading of the political setting of *A City Girl* that the reader recognizes the London presented in the fiction is not the London of 1887. As George has already given his vote and Arthur Grant is hoping for a Conservative victory then the events of the fiction take place in the London of either December 1885 or July 1886. While this could be merely an interesting note in a close reading of the fiction I would argue that recognizing the temporal setting will help readers understand why an author so closely involved in socialist politics at a time of political turbulence would produce a novel that entirely omits the socialist movement.

Both elections were held only months after the socialist movement was involved in two very large and well-reported disturbances, and in the case of the West End Riots socialists had hoped to begin the revolution and the dismantling of capitalism. If Arthur Grant's speech is delivered and George's vote cast during the December 1885 election then the Dod Street protest for free speech – attended by tens of thousands – is shown to have had no material or political effect on the inhabitants of Charlotte's Buildings. If both speech and vote are given during the July 1886 election then the West End Riots – which *The Times* described as 'the most alarming and destructive riot that has taken place in London for many years'[20] and which the leader of the SDF, Henry Mayers Hyndman, later recalled as generating a 'scare throughout London' among 'the rich classes' which was 'more cowardly and ridiculous than anything ever known in my day'[21] – had similarly made no impact on the politics of the workers. By presenting a London working-class population not only unaffected by recent events but apparently unconscious of them and maintaining allegiances to the older political parties, Harkness appears to present an image of socialist failure to the (implied) reader. But despite this image of socialism failing to reach the most needy in London, the reader is not encouraged to look to Arthur Grant and his Radical politics for change beneficial to the working class.

The Dangers of the Radical Narrative

In her article 'Space,' Marie-Laure Ryan sets out five levels (or, as she terms them, 'laminations') of space in the novel. These include the spaces where events take place, the general social and historical setting, the geographical

---

20 Editorial, *The Times*, 9 February 1886, p.9.
21 Henry Mayers Hyndman, *The Record of an Adventurous Life* (London: Macmillan, 1911), p.402.

area within which the story is enacted, the story world as completed by the reader's filling of spatial gaps and what she terms the 'Narrative Universe':

> the world (in the spatio-temporal sense of the term) presented as actual by the text, plus all the counterfactual worlds constructed by characters as beliefs, wishes, fears, speculations, hypothetical thinking, dreams and fantasies.[22]

What makes Arthur Grant dangerous – and by extension all Liberal-Radical politicians – is the fiction he and his political ideologies create to articulate and narrativize the 'working class'. Grant's understanding of the term 'the working class' is based on sentimentalist fantasies and creates an alternative world of 'East End London'. He imagines a world of equality based on the aesthetically pleasing external appearances of selected working-class people, judges others superficially and bases his political ideology on that superficial judgment. On meeting Nelly, he is stunned by her beauty and through this attraction he justifies his politics: 'He was wondering how a face like hers came to be in Whitechapel, and congratulating himself on this confirmation of his Radical opinions, for he believed that with the help of a good tailor, and a little polish, Whitechapel might sit down to dinner in Brook Street' (62). There is no depth to either Grant's attraction or his understanding of the yawning economic, social and cultural gap between the wealthy and the poor. Nor does he even recognize the working class as feeling human beings.

In his ideologically-driven fiction of the workers, emotions – and perhaps even consciousness – are associated only with the educated, aesthetic middle and upper class. His complacency over his affair with Nelly is based on the assumption that the working-class woman is emotionally unevolved: 'Intrigues with married ladies he knew to be dangerous; he quite forgot that "hands" have hearts' (78). And this assumption is extended to include the working-class male: 'He had thought that "hands" took babies as a matter of course; he had imagined that babies made very little difference to East End sweethearts' (125). This narrative of 'working class' had been justified to himself through a further assumption that honour was a quality unconnected with the workers. He assumed that, because George had not sought for him after Nelly's pregnancy was discovered, George (and working-class men generally) did not much care about illegitimate pregnancy, yet: 'the smile vanished when he realized that Nelly had kept his name secret – that

---

22 Marie-Laure Ryan, 'Space', in: Peter Hühn et al. (eds.), *The Living Handbook of Narratology* (Hamburg: Hamburg University), http://www.lhn.uni-hamburg.de/article/space, [accessed 23 Feb 2015].

she had tried to shield him from what she thought dangerous' (125). In this Radical fiction, working-class people are only acknowledged for their productive usefulness (hands) or noticed for their unexpected beauty (Nelly); fragmented and superficial bodies unencumbered with the higher human emotions inhabit his world of the worker.

While Arthur Grant's uninformed beliefs and assumptions of what is 'working class' might simply be read as the ideological gap between rich and poor, his association with Radical politics positions him as a warning against the claims that Radical politics adequately represents the working class in Parliament. The most powerful Liberal Radical at the end of the 1880s was Joseph Chamberlain. His tenure as Mayor in Birmingham in the 1870s had greatly extended the role of municipal government for the benefit of society and he carried that attitude to political involvement into his position as MP for Birmingham in the House of Commons. Chamberlain's peers, for instance fellow Liberal Lord Hartington, criticized his programme as socialist[23] and biographer Samuel Mencher claims that it 'incorporated the ideas of Henry George and the socialists and differed little, if at all, from the reforms supported by most labor and socialist leaders'.[24]

This similarity to the socialist programme would be expected to attract the votes of the enfranchised working-class male who was more comfortable with the established parties than the recently formed socialist groups. Hence in Harkness's novel George and Jack are aligned with the Conservative and Liberal parties respectively. But for the socialist author, the danger for the workers is that, despite superficial similarities with socialism, the Radicals worked for the perpetuation of capitalism and against the foundation of the socialist state with all its ambitions for true equality. The socialist mask worn by the Radical Liberals was created by men like Arthur Grant whose faulty understanding of the working class was built on the ideological fiction of the workers as happy in their ignorance and untroubled by the finer emotions of the wealthy. A political group making political decisions for a class of people imagined to be less (or un-) feeling, while apparently benign, is in effect a dangerous decoy away from the revolutionary goals of socialism. Liberal-Radical ideology places the interests of the wealthy front and centre of their politics. Nevertheless, this criticism should be read as levelled at Radical politics rather than the middle class as a flattened and homogenized social group.

---

23 Travis L. Crosby, *Joseph Chamberlain: A Most Radical Imperialist* (London: I. B. Tauris, 2011), p.52.
24 Samuel Mencher, *Poor Law to Poverty Program: Economic Security Policy in Britain and the United States* (Pittsburgh, PA: University of Pittsburg Press, 1968), p.184.

The fact that this novel (and most of Harkness's works of fiction) was published in bound form suggests that her intended reader would be a member of the concerned middle classes. The cost of the novel placed it beyond the reach of the ordinary working-class reader and in 1889 a reviewer in the 'Book Notes' column of Keir Hardie's *Labour Leader* thought the novel ought to be read 'by those who are alone able to solve the problem that the book presents'.[25] By presenting her political goals to the middle-class reader – no matter how open that reader is to those goals – appears to shift the responsibility for that change from the workers to others outside of that class. However, Harkness does not look solely to the wealthier classes to impose socialism onto the workers, rather she looks to socialists to work together, cross class, to bring about the socialist millennium.

This is most evident in her accounts of her work during the London dock strike of 1889 as she praises the combined skills of the working-class John Burns and Tom Mann, and the upper-class Henry Hyde Champion.[26] These are men who have acted together for the good of the workers; their class origins are unimportant. Beatrice Potter notes in her diary that '[t]he pictures she gives of Burns and Mann, of their hard work, single-mindedness and strain is very fine' and then, in typical Potter fashion, passive-aggressively questions her cousin's honesty: 'and it may be true'.[27] Similarly, the foundations of a labour party are presented as cross class as Harkness lists the organization of, and candidature for, parliamentary labour candidates as ranging from the working class (Burns again and James Keir Hardie) and the upper class (Champion again and Robert Cunninghame Graham).[28] Neither is class an issue when she recommends co-operation between socialists and the Salvation Army in the SDF's paper, *Justice* (owned by the upper-class Henry Mayers Hyndman and edited by the working-class Harry Quelch); rather, her concern is for a united group working together: 'For the army teaches us a great lesson. It has never split up. It is one large labour union'.[29] This call for a united socialist movement not present in reality means that the genre of literary realism is incapable of suggesting a positive way forward for socialists, but the embryonic literary modernism is potentially dangerous.

25   Quoted in Miller, p.95.

26   John Law, '"Salvation" and Socialism. In Praise of General Booth', *Pall Mall Gazette*, 21 October 1890, pp.1-2.

27   Norman and Jeanne Mackenzie eds. *The Diary of Beatrice Webb, Volume 1 1873-1892: Glitter Around and Darkness Within* (London: Virago, 1982), p.324.

28   Margaret G. [*sic*] Harkness, 'The Future of the Labour Party', *Pall Mall Gazette*, 7 March 1890, p.7.

29   Margaret E. Harkness, 'Salvationists and Socialists', *Justice*, 24 March 1888, p.2.

Arthur Grant's fiction of reality simultaneously romanticizes and fictionalizes his actions while oblivious to the destruction he causes in Nelly's life. Grant does express remorse for his actions but that remorse quickly turns into a fantasy that places him at the centre of the events:

> Of course he was dreadfully sorry. He tried to walk it off, to row it off, to drown it in champagne and whisky. That night tears came into his eyes when he looked at his West End baby. He was very proud of his tears – they were sentimental as those of a German lover. (122)

The 'German lover' is a reference to Goethe's story of Werther's doomed love for the beautiful peasant girl, Lotte in *The Sorrows of Young Werther* (1774) and Grant's positioning of himself, his life and his actions as those of a fictional protagonist represents the centrality and idealization of the individual self in Radical politics. Nelly – and the working class as a whole – cannot expect support from politicians who prioritize the individual (and particularly their individual self) over the collective. The association of Arthur Grant with proto-modernist literature is expanded beyond his fantasies of self as character and positions him as an author anticipating modernist fiction's concern with the internal and the psychological:

> He meant to start a novel when he came back to town, into which he would introduce some curious psychological studies he had come across, and some strange events. He would have no plot in it. Plots had gone out since the time of Thackeray and George Eliot. His novel should be a study of character, that is, an epitome of Arthur Grant. (77)

His ambitions for his fiction anticipate Virginia Woolf's rejection of the material focus of Edwardian literature and the 'moderns' recalibration of literary perspective onto 'the dark places of psychology'.[30] Grant – and Harkness – anticipate the new focus of literature but the association of Radical Arthur Grant with the interiority of the modernist novel acts as a warning against the Liberal-Radical claim to represent the workers in Parliament.

Neither realism with its suggestion of the eternal present nor the individualism of modernism could adequately present or broadcast the socialist seeds of hope. Therefore *A City Girl* is not limited to the single genre of realism; the pessimism of real socialist failure to reach the poorest must be moderated by the use of other literary genres.

---

30 Virginia Woolf, 'Modern Fiction', in *The Essays of Virginia Woolf, Volume 4: 1925-1928*, ed. by Andrew McNeille (London: Hogarth Press, 1984), pp.157-165 (p.162).

'The Old, Old Story': Sentimentalism, Melodrama and Tragedy

The relationship between literary realism and the working-class experience has long been seen as problematic. Although H. Gustav Klaus recognizes that realism, like everything else, is susceptible to change over time,[31] critics such as Pamela Fox and Ian Haywood argue that realism, a genre closely associated with the middle classes and the cult of individualism, cannot adequately convey the working-class experience.[32] In his essay 'Margaret Harkness and the Socialist Novel', John Goode argues that William Morris's and George Bernard Shaw's avoidance of realism 'responds to the fact that realism is not available to socialist writers in its classic form because it assumes that reality is merely to be perceived and not made'.[33] The literary articulation of working-class experience was not simply an alternative aesthetic endeavour but one which had a dual intent: to contest the dominant, bourgeois, capitalist ideology that places the workers in the situations they present and are struggling to escape in reality, and also 'to effect a change in the recipient's consciousness'.[34] Creative literature has a long tradition in the presentation of both working-class life and radical politics, and the aims of both the working-class and socialist (of whatever class origin) authors are similar: to present an alternative perspective on the world in order to change the perceptions of the reader and, through the reader, to effect material change. For Harkness, at this point, the engine for change was socialism; and as socialism did not appear to be driving that change forward then the genre of realism needed modifying.

Like many socialist and working-class authors Harkness builds *A City Girl* through the interleaving of a number of literary genres. Although a manipulated realism is useful for the social and political spaces of the fiction, the lives and relationships of the individual characters are presented through other genres. The beautiful, working-class Nelly Ambrose and handsome,

---

31   H. Gustav Klaus, 'Introduction', in *The Socialist Novel in Britain*, ed. H. Gustav Klaus (Brighton: Harvester Press, 1982), pp.1-6 (p.2).

32   See Ian Haywood, *Working-Class Fiction from Chartism to* Trainspotting (Plymouth: Northcote House, 1997); Pamela Fox, *Class Fictions: Shame and Resistance in the British Working-Class Novel, 1890-1945* (Burham, NC: Duke University Press, 1994).

33   John Goode, 'Margaret Harkness and the Socialist Novel', in H. Gustav Klaus (ed.), *The Socialist Novel in Britain* (Brighton: Harvester Press, 1982), pp.43-66 (p.46).

34   Pauline Johnson, *Marxist Aesthetics: The foundations with everyday life for an emancipated consciousness* (Abingdon: Routledge, 2013), p.1.

middle-class Arthur Grant are categorized through literary genre as Engels describes their relationship as 'the old, old story, the proletarian girl seduced by a middle-class man'. Thus the realism of the novel is overlapped with the romance plot of emotional relationships and the class- and gender-based power imbalances of melodrama. This amalgamation of genres mitigates the excesses of each: realism damps down any suggestion or hope of a successful conclusion for Nelly and Arthur's potentially idealized inter-class relationship, as neither character considers the long-term continuation of their affair. Romance softens the hard edges of the melodrama plot: Nelly is not the innocent, pursued maiden – she is neither tricked nor forced into the affair – but instead she is the 'Masher of the Buildings' whose paid employment gives her the freedom to 'come and go at all hours of the day and night without comment' (74); Arthur is not the heartless and deliberate villain but rather a self-centred and thoughtless man who forgets that '"hands" have hearts' (78). Nelly is aware that Grant is married so the purity of their emotions is compromised and the melodramatic imbalance of power less pronounced as they both enter the affair with a degree of realism about the situation. Ruth Livesey, in *Socialism, Sex and the Culture of Aestheticism in Britain*, reads the socialist romance genre as 'the narrative of hope,'[35] but Harkness's swirl of genres negates this forward projection of hope and grounds both her characters and reader in the problems of her present. While the imbrication of realism, romance and melodrama tempers the latter two genres' potential flights of fancy to present a fairly clear-eyed view of the affair, she further anchors her characters to the real by introducing the motifs of both sensation fiction and naturalism as Nelly's paternity is questioned.

Nelly's relationship with her mother and brother is presented as difficult and abusive primarily because she stands apart from her family through both superior physical appearance and personality. The reason for this difference may be paternity:

> Her mother could perhaps have told why she and Tom [Nelly's brother] were so very different; could have said whence she inherited the ways and looks which caused her to be called the Masher of the Buildings. But her mother kept her secret, if she had one to keep. Nelly was only aware that her mother had been a lady's maid before she married a pale, consumptive invalid; an invalid Nelly had called father, until a hearse carried him away from the Buildings, and Tom took his place in the wooden arm-chair and behind the shop-counter. (74)

Thus it is suggested that Nelly may be the biological child of an upper-

---

35 Ruth Livesey, *Socialism, Sex and the Culture of Aestheticism in Britain, 1880-1914* (Oxford: Oxford University Press, 2007), p.71.

class father, someone other than the father of her brother. But rather than following this motif of sensationalism through to the usual conclusion of individual salvation (Nelly) by another (her biological father), Harkness leaves this thread untied and takes a nurture-over-nature approach. Nelly – regardless of her parentage – suffers the same deprivations, temptations and punishments as any other working-class girl in her position. Harkness presents no inherent morality or sensibility, parentage has no effect on the material life lived under capitalism, nor does she invoke the *deus ex machina* of sensation fiction: no rich relative swoops out of the wings to save anyone from trouble or danger.

The anti-realist, sometimes awkward, technique of the *deus* was used by Chartist authors earlier in the century, according to Rob Breton, to expose the hypocrisies of a society simultaneously preaching the gospel of self help while closing down opportunities for social mobility. He argues that: 'The machina expresses a will to agency by demonstrating the very political, economic, social, and even cultural frustrations to agency … it confirms the restrictions imposed on working-class agency by making visible the failures of fallback support networks – of the church, government, indeed all institutions within the market system.'[36] By raising the suggestion of a wealthy, upper-class paternity and then leaving that image to twist in the air, Harkness addresses the limitations of working-class life. Already beset by economic restrictions through capitalism, Nelly cannot expect a *deus*, or rather what Breton terms a *homo ex machina*,[37] to appear out of the institutions of family, marriage or religion: not only will no rich relative save the day, no spurned lover will legitimize her status as a mother, no Catholic church will offer her emotional comfort or financial support.

Entrapped by the same or similar 'political, economic, social, and even cultural frustrations to agency' Breton recognizes as encircling the Chartist male, the restrictive nature of Nelly's situation draws on the pessimism of naturalism and is reinforced by her questionable paternity. Ingrid von Rosenberg notes that Harkness is utilizing the genre in her fiction at a very early stage in English naturalism: she is writing 'almost as early as George Moore, who is commonly regarded as Zola's first British disciple'.[38] Naturalism's interest in the hereditary propensities passed through the generations (for instance, Zola's tracing of hysteria and alcoholism through the Rougon-Macquart family) is raised through the implication that Nelly's

---

36 Rob Breton, 'Ghosts in the Machina: Plotting in Chartist and Working-Class Fiction', *Victorian Studies*, (2005) 557-575 (p.562).
37 *Ibid*, p.560.
38 Rosenberg, p.155.

superiority and unusual love of cleanliness is inherited from someone other than her grubby, alcoholic mother. Less positively, Nelly's implied illegitimate birth is also repeated in the actual illegitimacy of her own child.

Again, the use of naturalism is tempered by other genres drawn into the fiction: unlike other English naturalist authors, Harkness does not present working-class life as something to be endlessly endured (George Gissing *passim*) or only escaped through death (for instance, Arthur Morrison's Dicky Perrott in the 1896 novel *A Child of the Jago*). Instead she presents the happiest ending possible under current social, political and economic conditions as Nelly and George reunite after the death of her baby and plan their future together as a married couple working for 'a society, or a club ... made up of people who write books' who have got 'a lot of little cottages, about an hour out of London' and want 'some one to look after the gardens, and ... some one else to look after the servants' (130). Although their lives will be improved through lighter work, friendly employers and life outside of the inner city slums, their agency is not increased. They maintain their position as employees under capitalism and, although Nelly moves into a managerial role 'look[ing] after the servants,' under Marxist economics she is downgraded from a producer (as she was when employed as a seamstress) to the non-productive labour of domestic service. Nelly's downward trajectory in terms of her autonomy begins with her removal from the labour force when her employer discovers her pregnancy. Removed from useful, productive labour through social stigma – dismissed from her employment because 'only "honest" women should make trousers for virtuous sweaters' (93) – rather than the advances in mechanical production Marx saw as the problem, she becomes a member of a 'larger and larger part of the working class to be employed unproductively'.[39]

Nelly's removal from the productive workforce inhibits her freedom as she loses her economic independence, now unable to earn her 'pound a week ... sometimes two-and-twenty shillings' because she had the skill to 'machine the buttons' (63). Economic independence bought her physical and emotional freedom: 'In the East End girls come and go at all hours of the day and night without comment, especially "hands," like Nelly, who help to pay the rent' (74). In this way Nelly enacts the arguments of the feminist socialists that working-class women held a more emancipated position than their middle- or upper-class counterparts because they possessed economic autonomy. Annie Besant counters Ernest Belfort Bax's (rather astonishing)

---

39 Karl Marx, *Capital: Volume 1*, trans. Ben Fowkes (London: Penguin, 1990), p.574.

claims that all women are at heart 'an amplified, beautified, embellished sexual organ' who benefit from their dependent position by taking the 'lion's share at the banquet of life' and want the vote only 'to get infamous laws passed against men *as* men',[40] on a class basis:

> If Mr. Bax were in the habit of associating with working women he would find that sex is a much less prominent matter with them than among the women of his own social grade; the business of life, the interests outside the home, have educated the former in to human beings.[41]

Nelly's role as worker gives her a certain freedom through her income but under capitalism her dependency on employment by others places this freedom in a tenuous position. The powerful forces of capitalism and patriarchy are brought to bear on her when she transgresses the social restrictions placed on sexual activity. Despite her economic parity with working-class men, Nelly's gender is her downfall in the way that Eleanor Marx and Edward Aveling note gender disparity in their essay 'The Woman Question':

> Society provides, recognises, legalizes for [men] the means of gratifying the sex instinct. In the eyes of that same society an unmarried woman who acts after the fashion habitual to her unmarried brothers and the men that dance with her at balls, or work with her in the shop, is a pariah.[42]

Because *A City Girl* was published around the time Harkness was associated with the SDF, she would have been surrounded by the debates on women's position in both society and the group. As Karen Hunt notes, for many SDF members there was a clear gendered division between male socialists and their wives, the latter 'were to be congratulated on their acquiescence, self-sacrifice, toleration and lack of domestic opposition'[43] as their husbands carried out their SDF work. Similarly, even during her period of financial autonomy Nelly fulfills the female-gendered domestic duties: she enters the story carrying 'a large market basket' (45) as she returns from the weekly shopping trip and prepares breakfast for her sleeping mother and brother (51). While there were arguments within the SDF against paid female labour because of the 'deleterious effect of work on women workers

---

40   Ernest Belfort Bax, 'Some Heterodox Notes on the Woman Question', *To-Day*, July (1887), 24-32 (p.24, p.29, p.32).

41   Annie Besant, 'Misogyny in Excelsis', *To-Day*, August (1887), 51-56 (p.54).

42   Edward Aveling and Eleanor Marx, 'The Woman Question', *Westminster Review*, 1886, in *Marxists Internet Archive*, transcribed by Sally Ryan, 2000, marxists.org, [accessed 17 January 2015].

43   Karen Hunt, *Equivocal Feminists: The Social Democratic Federation and the Woman Question, 1884-1911* (Cambridge: Cambridge University Press, 1996), p.92.

themselves'[44] these concerns were, as Hunt notes, used as part of the general argument that working women impacted negatively on the employment of working men. But Harkness shows the reader that poor women laboured under the dual pressures of 'visible' paid work and 'invisible' domestic work:

> The wives of these men [casual labourers] added to the family income by charing, tailoring and sack-making, besides doing all the house-work. They were little better than beasts of burden, poor things, for East End husbands have but a low opinion of the weaker sex. (44)

> Saturday [was] the hardest day of all the week for East End wives and mothers. To rise early and go to bed late was the Saturday rule of women in the Buildings. They must clean their "place," get the children's clothes ready for Sunday, scrub, cook, and bake, whilst boys and girls hung about and husbands did nothing. (44)

Once her non-domestic work – and therefore financial autonomy – is removed by the termination of her employment, Nelly is reduced to dependency on the men in her life: beaten and evicted by her brother, she is taken to the Salvation Army rescue rooms by George and handed to Captain Lobe who assigns her a home with a female sergeant for which George pays the rent. Although George is not described as a violent man (rather his reunion with Nelly after the death of the baby presents him as a forgiving man) he is also figured as conservative. His support for the Conservative Party is combined with a very clear sense of gendered roles: in his conversation with Captain Lobe about the female members of the Salvation Army he states, "Well, I'm all for women keeping quiet myself" (100). And while the reader follows Nelly through her maturity from a vain girl to an experienced and worldly mother there is no indication that George will or can similarly develop his character. George's oft-repeated lament, 'I wish I'd never left the Service', portrays him as backward-looking, not only in his comfort in the known of the past but also his desire to devolve the responsibility for his own life to others. 'In the Service he had had no vote; he had been forbidden to marry; his work had been fixed' (59) and his longing for a return to this state of infantilization[45] and desire for certainty about gendered roles does not predict an easy future for Nelly as his wife.

So could this closing-down of Nelly's future through the massive pressures of capitalism and patriarchy be read as a tragedy as well as the pessimism of naturalism? Nelly's hubris – both her excessive pride in her looks and her

---

44 *Ibid*, p.121.
45 Rob Breton, 'The Sentimental Socialism of Margaret Harkness', *English Language Notes*, 48.1, (2010) 27-39 (p.30).

delight in the affair with Arthur Grant – is punished excessively through the death of her baby and her imprisonment through marriage, which might be read as a living death for her. If we take this approach and apply Raymond Williams's reading of tragedy, we are then offered a way out of the dead-end of naturalism. Williams argues that readers need to widen their response to tragedy, to stop 'confin[ing] our attention to the hero' and therefore 'confining ourselves to one kind of experience'. That life carries on 'after so important a death' is seen as part of the tragedy but, he argues, '[w]hat is involved, of course, is not a simple forgetting, or a picking-up for the new day. The life that is continued is informed by the death; has indeed, in a sense, been created by it.'[46] Nelly survives but the life that continues is informed by her experiences and projected out of the fiction to the reader with the aim of engendering material change in the world outside of the novel. Her burial in domestic servitude should be unfavourably compared to her freedom through employment and the world surrounding the reader needs to be re-ordered to remove dependency on others: both female dependency on the male and the worker's dependency on employers.

Margaret Harkness: Paternalist, Salvationist or Socialist?

John Goode's summary of Harkness's personality describes her as either 'a woman of consistent ideas who worked opportunistically in a series of alliances (her own image of herself), a radical feminist converted to socialism in the mid-1880s and disillusioned by it in the early 1890s, or simply a neurotic of wide but volatile sympathies vacillating between seeing herself as a journalist in pursuit of "cold-blooded copy" and a rejected saviour of the working class'.[47] But posterity's record of Harkness's personality has been coloured by her estrangement from Beatrice Potter and Potter's description of her cousin in her diaries. Perhaps we might be a little cautious of Potter's description as possibly overly critical: this is the woman who recorded Eleanor Marx as having 'ugly features and expression, and complexion showing the signs of an unhealthy excited life, kept up with stimulants and tempered with narcotics'.[48] Perhaps we should focus on Potter's early description of the differences between herself and her cousin in their attitude to life and individual suffering. Potter recorded of Harkness:

> She attaches much more importance to individuals, resenting what she has nicknamed 'my phantom theory.' She won't admit that persons, past and

46   Raymond Williams, *Modern Tragedy* (Toronto: Broadview, 2006) p.79.
47   Goode, 'Margaret Harkness and the Socialist Novel', p.52.
48   Webb, *Diaries*, p.88.

present, are as it were groups of qualities, bound up for the time in one form – this form perishing, the qualities alone being persistent ... Her mind naturally seizes upon and magnifies the characteristics of persons and the peculiar nature of their surroundings.[49]

For a woman who sympathizes with the suffering of the individual, the impersonal and theoretical attitude of her cousin (who will become an important voice for Fabian socialism) and the Marxist economics of the SDF must be frustratingly alienated from human suffering. Her detailed knowledge of working-class destitution could not allow her to be comfortable with Quelch's reply to her article 'Salvationists and Socialists', claiming that 'it is very questionable if it [feeding the poor] does not ultimately aggravate the evils it aims at remedying'.[50] Her work with the poor individualized and humanized their suffering and this makes the theoretical arguments of the Fabians and SDF unpalatable.

The work of the Salvation Army, on the other hand, is viewed on a human level, but Kevin Swafford reads this as evidence of Harkness's paternalism in his study of her next novel, *Out of Work*. He argues that this 'novel seems to envision *socialism as something bestowed, a gift from the enlightened moral leaders of the ruling classes*'.[51] Between the expensive bound publication of her fiction and her praise for the work of the Salvation Army in the slums of London there is much to support this argument of paternalism. However, Harkness does not prioritize one movement over the other; rather she urges both socialists and Salvationists to 'work more together than they do at present, for they have many points of common interest'.[52] In the novel, Captain Lobe saves Nelly from destitution and possible death but his actions are similar to those of the Radical politicians, albeit more humane and sympathetic: he rescues the individual. Only a reorganization of society on socialist lines will prevent the destitution of future 'Nellys' but the Salvation Army has no interest in promoting or developing socialist change. For Harkness, the Salvation Army deals with the present and immediate suffering while the socialists work towards a future where the Army's services will not be necessary. The expansion of the franchise to parts of the working-class male population in 1867 and 1884 meant that hope for future change did not need to originate outside of the working class and, therefore, working-class and socialist fiction at the end of the century was not restricted to 'endings

49 Webb, *Diaries*, p.80.
50 Editor's Reply, 'Salvationists and Socialists', *Justice*, 24 March 1888, p.2.
51 Swafford, p.47. Original italics.
52 Harkness, 'Salvationists and Socialists', p.2.

that only resolve by way of outside forces'.[53] Engels's criticism of the role of the Salvation Army in *A City Girl* is understandable until Harkness's concerns for both the immediate and long-term well-being of the poor is recognized, along with her desire to marry socialist goals with human empathy.

Her dislike of revolutionary politics meant that her inclination leant towards ethical socialism, but that did not rise until the early 1890s with the Independent Labour Party and the Clarion group. By that time she was – and had been – alienated from those with whom she had worked in the past. In 1887 she could not see the socialist movement having made any progress over the previous few years (regardless of the events of Dod Street and the West End Riots) and this is indicated through the complex temporal scheme and generic make-up of *A City Girl*. The Salvation Army is not the way forward but a safety net for those in dire need. What the reader is presented with in this novel is a plea to reconsider the superficial sympathies of Radical Liberal politicians and for the sympathetic middle-class reader to throw their weight behind the – as yet ineffective – socialists for a multi-class effort to change the world for the better.

---

53   Breton, 'Ghosts in the Machina', p.560.

BIOGRAPHY OF MARGARET HARKNESS

Deborah Mutch and Terry Elkiss

'John Law' was the pseudonym of Margaret Elise Harkness, daughter of Robert Harkness (1826-1886), a Church of England clergyman and rector of Wimborne St. Giles, Dorset, and his wife Elizabeth Bolton Toswill (neé Seddon, 1824[1]-1916). Margaret was born in Great Malvern on 28 February 1854 and christened on 7 July of that year. She was educated at home but was sent to the Stirling House finishing school in Bournemouth in 1875 at the same time as Beatrice Webb (neé Potter, 1858-1943), her second cousin on her mother's side, where the girls became close friends despite their differences in age and wealth. The two remained in contact and socialized after both moved to London and Margaret was probably the 'intimate friend' with whom Beatrice lived in Bavaria in 1884 after the latter's relationship with Joseph Chamberlain had ended.

Harkness resisted her family's pressure to marry well, early on indicating her repugnance to marriage, and determined to live independently in order to leave the repressive and intellectually stifling confines of her family. Nevertheless, her parents supported her – albeit reluctantly – as she began training as a nurse in 1877 at Westminster Hospital. After a brief return home for apparent health reasons, she went back to London in 1878, but 'her people' now opposed her staying at Westminster and even encouraged her to become a governess. Rejecting this advice, she began an apprenticeship as a dispenser in 1878, worked in the dispensary at Guy's Hospital in 1880 and in 1882 she nursed Beatrice's mother, Laurencina Potter, during her final illness. However, she told Beatrice that she had no love of nursing and was more interested in her patients' political views than their illnesses.

Her ambition turned towards authorship as a career and her decision to earn money by writing and journalism caused a rift with her family. This initially left her dependent upon financial aide from the Potters, most probably from Beatrice's father, Richard, a wealthy businessman. One of her first steps in her writing career was to apply for a Reader's Pass at the

---

1   Joyce Bellamy's notes for Margaret Harkness's entry in the *Dictionary of Labour Biography* record Elizabeth Bolton Harkness's year of birth as 1821 but Census figures give 1824.

British Museum Library Reading Room in 1880, six years before Beatrice. Her first signed publication was 'Women as Civil Servants' in the periodical *Nineteenth Century* in 1881 and she began to publish articles and books on subjects as widely disparate as railway labour, Egyptian history and municipal government in London. In addition to her writing and research, she presented a course of lectures at the British Museum on the ancient Assyrians, with the encouragement of distinguished British Museum scholar, R. Stuart Poole, which subsequently provided the basis for her book, *Assyrian Life and History* (1883).

Around the early 1880s she began to take an active interest in the suffering of the working class and in politics as a way to alleviate or eradicate that suffering, expanding upon ideas that she had earlier broached in her private correspondence with Beatrice. It was Harkness who recommended Beatrice to some of the most influential women of the socialist movement – Eleanor Marx, Annie Besant, Olive Schreiner, Amy Levy – and who introduced Beatrice to her future husband, Sidney Webb. At some time between 1885 and 1887 Harkness was involved with the Social Democratic Federation (SDF) but her association was short-lived, as she recounts in an article for the *Star* in 1889 that she 'discovered it to be a dead body in a few months'. Through her brief connection she met and later worked with Henry Hyde Champion, Tom Mann, Ben Tillett and John Burns as they helped organize London's Great Dock Strike of 1889 for which she is credited as involving Cardinal Manning to negotiate a successful conclusion. Her work behind the scenes included soliciting support and funds for the dock workers and their families, as well as playing an advisory role at meetings of the strike committee, but this work is rarely acknowledged.

At this time she was also involved in Champion's periodical, the *Labour Elector*, and in a confidential note by Mann to Burns, he recommended that 'Miss Harkness should be on the LEC (Labour Elector Committee) ... I know she will like to be if we are willing'. However, Mann's main concern was that Champion might object because he knew Harkness was 'opposed to any money transaction of a shaky nature' that might arise. Possibly, her association with Champion in the questionable financing of James Keir Hardie's 1888 Mid Lanark parliamentary election bid – what became known as the 'Tory Gold' scandal – had left her wary of such schemes, but not of Champion himself.

Although she had disapproved of the SDF's shift towards revolutionary socialism after the West End Riots of February 1886 and the Trafalgar Square demonstrations of November 1887, she was similarly critical of trade unions as a mechanism for change and promoted the development of a parliamentary labour party. It was around this period of involvement with socialist politics that she produced her series of social condition novels: *A City Girl* (1887) – the novel which generated Engels's famous definition of realism – *Out of Work* (1888), *Captain Lobe: A Story of the Salvation Army* (1889) and *A Manchester Shirtmaker* (1890).

In 1890, shortly after the conclusion of the dock strike, Harkness travelled to Germany and Austria to study labour conditions but an undisclosed illness forced her to return to Britain. The following year she travelled to the Australia and New Zealand, arriving in Australia a few months after Champion had left. It is possible that she was working for the *Pall Mall Gazette* during this trip. It has also been claimed that she travelled to the United States, but the source of that claim has not been documented. On her return to Britain at the end of 1891 she began editing *Tinsley's Magazine* (with which Champion was now associated) and in April 1891 *Tinsley's* became the short-lived *Novel Review* under her direction and apparent ownership. She was forced, probably through a combination of ill health and financial losses, to give up the editorship of the *Novel Review* in July 1892 and the journal ceased publication in December of the same year. She also serialized 'Roses and Crucifix' in the *Woman's Herald* between 5 December 1891 and 27 February 1892). She renewed her association with Champion's *Labour Elector*, which was now being edited by Michael Maltman Barry, and she began serializing 'Connie' in June 1893 but it remained incomplete when the periodical folded in early 1894.

That same year she returned to Australia where she acted as the foreign correspondent from London for the *Fortnightly Review*. By October 1895 she was resident in Coolgardie, Western Australia, where she met with the Irish revolutionary and land reformer Michael Davitt during his speaking tour and she claimed to have financially supported both Champion and the *Labour Elector* with her inheritance. It is here that she serialized 'Called to the Bar: A Coolgardie Novel' in the Perth *Western Mail* between July and September 1897 and privately published *Imperial Credit* in 1899, which was printed by the prestigious Adelaide publisher Vardon and Pritchard. She also began a regular column for the Perth *West Australian* in 1903. Harkness departed from Australia in 1904, returning to Britain at the end of the year where she published *George Eastmont, Wanderer* (1905) before leaving Britain again on the S. S. Golconda for Madras on 17 February 1905. Letters sent between the period 1906 and 1912 place her in Madras, Calcutta and Columbo where she continued to publish articles for the *West Australian*, travel books and a novel,

The Horoscope (1914), having engaged James B. Pinker as her London literary agent. She renewed her acquaintance with former SDF member Annie Besant who had moved to India in 1893.

Harkness returned to Britain before 1914 and nursed her mother through her final illness in 1916. It was during this period that she became estranged from her brother William, removing the dedication to him in the reissue of *Captain Lobe* (having reverted to her original title) in 1915, and began the arrangements for a memorial window in Wimborne St Giles dedicated to her parents. After the death of her mother she indicated she was returning to France to undertake undisclosed work. She published her final novel, *A Curate's Promise: a story of Three Weeks, September 14-October 5 1917* in 1921 and died in the modest Pensione Castagnoli in Florence on 10 December 1923. She was buried the following day in the local Allori Cemetery in a 'tomba di seconda classe' and simply identified on her death certificate as a spinster of independent means.

Bibliography

Bellamy, Joyce and Beate Kaspar, 'Harkness, Margaret Elise (1854-1923), Socialist Author and Journalist', in Joyce Bellamy and John Saville, *Dictionary of Labour Biography*, vol. 8 (London: Macmillan, 1987), pp.103-113.

Elkiss, Terry, *A Law unto Herself: The Hidden Life of Margaret Elise Harkness, Author, Activist, and Adventurer* (manuscript in preparation).

Kapp, Yvonne, *Eleanor Marx, Vol. II The Crowded Years (1884-1898)* (London: Lawrence and Wishart, 1976).

Lucas, John, 'Harkness, Margaret Elise (1854–1923)', *Oxford Dictionary of National Biography*, Oxford University Press, 2004; online edn, May 2005 [http://www.oxforddnb.com/view/article/56894, accessed 23 May 2011].

Mackenzie, Norman, ed., *The Letters of Sidney and Beatrice Webb: I Apprenticeships, 1873-1892* (Cambridge: Cambridge University Press, 1978).

Mackenzie, Norman and Jeanne, eds., *The Diary of Beatrice Webb, Vol. 1 1873-1892: Glitter Around and Darkness Within* (London: Virago, 1982).

Nord, Deborah Epstein, *Walking the Victorian Streets: Women, Representation and the City* (Ithaca, NY: Cornell University Press, 1995).

CHRONOLOGY OF MARGARET HARKNESS

Deborah Mutch and Terry Elkiss

1854: Harkness born 28 February Great Malvern, Worcestershire.

1875: Sent to finishing school at Stirling House, Bournemouth.

1877: Begins nurse training at Westminster Hospital, London.

1878: Begins training as dispenser.

1880: Works in dispensary at Guy's Hospital; applies for Reader's Pass for the Reading Room at the British Library.

1881: First publication: 'Women as Civil Servants', *Nineteenth Century*, September issue – as Margaret E. Harkness.

1882: Nurses Laurencina Potter, mother of Beatrice, during last illness.

1883: Publishes *Assyrian Life and History* with the Religious Tract society's By-Paths of Bible Knowledge.

1884: Publishes *Egyptian Life and History according to the Monuments* with the Religious Tract society's By-Paths of Bible Knowledge; accompanies Beatrice Potter to Bavaria.

31 May–19 July 1886: Lives at Katherine Buildings, Whitechapel 'for purpose of observation'.

c.1885–1887: At some point becomes affiliated with, and possibly a member of, the Social Democratic Federation.

1887: Publishes *A City Girl* with Henry Vizetelly.

7 October 1887–20 April 1888: Probable editor and contributor to the series 'Tempted London' in *British Weekly*.

6 April–14 December 1888: 'Captain Lobe: a story of the East End' serialized in *British Weekly*.

13 April–28 December 1888: Editor and possibly author of the series 'Tempted London: Young Women' in *British Weekly.*

1888: Publishes *Out of Work* with Swan Sonnenschein.

1889: Publishes *Captain Lobe: A Story of the Salvation Army* with Hodder and Stoughton; involved in London dock strike, 12 August–14 September.

1890: Publishes *A Manchester Shirtmaker: a realistic story of to-day* with Authors' Co-operative Publishing Company; introduces Beatrice Potter to Sidney Webb; visits Germany and Austria to study labour conditions but undisclosed illness forces return home.

1891: New edition of *Captain Lobe* published under the title *In Darkest London* with an introduction by General Booth; resumes travels, visits New Zealand, Australia, and possibly the United States; assumed editorship and possible ownership of *Tinsley's Magazine*, renamed *The Novel Review*, which ceased publication in December 1892.

5 December 1891–27 February 1892: 'Roses and Crucifix' serialized in *Woman's Herald.*

1893: *In Darkest London* reissued with a dedication to brother William Bathurst Harkness; returns to Australia, visiting a co-operative labour settlement, Pitt Town, in February.

June 1893-January 1894: Publishes 'Connie' in Henry Hyde Champion's *Labour Elector* but periodical folds before completion.

1895-96: Establishes herself in Coolgardie, Western Australia for research; opens a typewriting office.

30 July–24 September 1897: Serializes 'Called to the Bar: A Coolgardie Novel' in *Western Mail*, Perth.

1899: Publication of *Imperial Credit* in Perth through Vardon and Pritchard.

1903-04: Becomes feature reporter for the *West Australian*, Perth, contributing a weekly column, 'The Passing Hour', as well as regular news articles.

1904: Departs Australia, arrives in London 1904/05 where she writes a 'London Letter' for the *West Australian.*

1905: Publishes *George Eastmont, Wanderer* in London with Burns and Oates;

travels from London to Madras on S. S. Golconda.

1905–7: Writes a series of travels accounts and news reports on Ceylon and India for the *West Australian*.

1909: Publishes *Glimpses of Hidden India* with Thacker, Spink & Co. of Calcutta.

1912: Reports to her London literary agent that she has completed the novel, *The Editor of the Daily News* but the manuscript has not survived; revised edition of *Glimpses of Hidden India* under the new title *Indian Snapshots* with Thacker, Spink Co. of Calcutta.

1914: Publishes *Modern Hyderabad* with Thacker, Spink & Co. of Calcutta; publishes *The Horoscope* simultaneously in Calcutta and London; possibly returns to Britain this year.

1915: Estrangement from brother William; reprint of *Captain Lobe* with dedication to William removed.

1916: Nurses mother through final illness.

1917: Contacts the rector of Wimborne St. Giles to establish a memorial for her parents, notes her dissatisfaction with her brother William in this regard and indicates that she must soon return to France for unidentified work.

1921: Publishes *A Curate's Promise: a story of Three Weeks, September 14-October 5 1917* in London through Hodder and Stoughton.

10 December 1923: Dies at Pensione Castagnoli, Florence and is buried in the Allori Cemetery.

1934: Installation of a window dedicated to her parents at Wimborne St Giles donated by Harkness.

SUGGESTIONS FOR FURTHER READING

Barnes, John, *Socialist Champion: Portrait of the Gentleman as Crusader* (Melbourne: Australian Scholarly Publishing, 2006)

Bellamy, Joyce and Beate Kaspar, 'Harkness, Margaret Elise (1854-1923), Socialist Author and Journalist', in *Dictionary of Labour Biography*, vol. 8, Joyce Bellamy and John Saville (eds), (Basingstoke: Macmillan, 1987), pp.103-113

Hapgood, Lynne, '"Is This Friendship?" Eleanor Marx, Margaret Harkness and the Idea of Socialist Community', in *Eleanor Marx (1855-1898): Life, Work, Contacts*, ed. by John Stokes (Aldershot: Ashgate, 2000), pp.129-143

Kapp, Yvonne, *Eleanor Marx, Vol. II The Crowded Years (1884-1898)* (London: Lawrence and Wishart, 1976)

Kirwan, Bernadette, 'Introduction', in Margaret Harkness *Out of Work* (London: Merlin, 1990), pp.v-xix

Lucas, John 'Harkness, Margaret Elise (1854–1923)', *Oxford Dictionary of National Biography*, Oxford University Press, 2004; online edn, May 2005, http://www.oxforddnb.com/view/article/56894 [accessed 23 May 2011]

Mackenzie, Norman (ed.), *The Letters of Sidney and Beatrice Webb: I Apprenticeships, 1873-1892* (Cambridge: Cambridge University Press, 1978)

— and Jeanne Mackenzie, (eds), *The Diary of Beatrice Webb, Vol. 1 1873-1892: Glitter Around and Darkness Within* (London: Virago, 1982)

Motte, Brunhild de la, 'Radicalism – feminism – socialism: the case of the women novelists', in *The Rise of Socialist Fiction, 1880-1914* (Brighton: Harvester, 1987), pp.28-48

Nord, Deborah Epstein, *Walking the Victorian Streets: Women, Representation and the City* (Ithica, NY: Cornell University Press, 1995)

Vicinus, Martha, *Independent Women: Work and Community for Single Women, 1850-1920* (Chicago: University of Chicago Press, 1985)

Walkowitz, Judith R., *City of Dreadful Delight: Narratives of Sexual Danger in Late-Victorian London* (London: Virago, 1994)

A NOTE ON THE TEXT

A City Girl was originally published by Vizetelly & Co., London in 1887 (who were also the first to publish Emile Zola's fiction in Britain) and a second edition was produced by the Author's Co-operative Publishing Co., London in 1890 as a shilling imprint. The text for this edition is taken from the original Vizetelly publication and the minor changes made to the Author's Co-operative edition are recorded in the footnotes. Both editions were published under the pseudonym 'John Law'. Any obvious errors have been silently corrected.

ACKNOWLEDGEMENTS

All research projects are collaborative at heart and the work for this project has been no different. I am thankful to my institution, De Montfort University in Leicester, UK, for awarding teaching relief and giving me the time and intellectual space to complete the project. I would also like to extend many thanks to all the presenters and delegates who attended 'In Harkness' London': a symposium on the life and work of Margaret Harkness, held at Birkbeck University, 22 November 2014, for all the lively debates on Harkness and her work. Particular thanks must go to the organizers, Dr. Ana Parejo Vadillo, Flore Janssen and Lisa Robertson for bringing together so many Harkness enthusiasts for such an enlightening day. The introduction for this edition benefitted greatly from insightful comments by Lisa, Flore and Terry Elkiss. Enormous thanks are also due to the tenacious – and incredibly modest – Terry, without whom the timeline and biography of Harkness would have been significantly truncated and, in some areas, mistaken. His willingness to share his fascinating and important findings is truly socialistic. The magnificent Catherine Pope has demonstrated the patience of a saint during this project, providing calm and insightful support during the bumps along the way. In the background of this project the Dawson-Edwards branch of my family tree have cheered me on, excitedly awaiting the debut of 'Granny in the big hat' as the cover girl of this book. And, quietly, uncomplainingly, David Ellis keeps everything going so I have the luxury of burying myself in my work. Without him, none of this would have happened.

ABOUT THE EDITOR

Deborah Mutch is a Senior Lecturer in the Department of English at De Montfort University, Leicester, UK. Her primary field of research is the fiction published by the British socialist movement at the end of the nineteenth and beginning of the twentieth centuries. She has published widely in this area including articles on authors such as Robert Blatchford, A. Neil Lyons and Charles Allen Clarke in journals including *Literature and History*, *Nineteenth Century Studies* and *Victorian Periodicals Review*. She is the editor of *British Socialist Action, 1884-1914* (Pickering & Chatto) and *English Socialist Periodicals, 1880-1900* (Ashgate).

DEDICATION

For Katherine Margaret (Meg) Dawson (1912-1993), Grace Britton, Anne Buck, Elizabeth Mutch and Christine Mountain, respectively daughters and grand-daughters of Eliza Edwards (neé Anderson) whose dreamy, youthful face looks back at us from the cover. Without all of these inspirational women this edition would literally not have been possible.

A City Girl

Dedicated to Andor, Count Szechényi[1]

1 Possibly Andor Szechényi (1865-1907). Szechényi was a renowned traveller who may possibly have visited Britain during the period Harkness was writing the novel. He was also the grandson of Hungarian Count Count István Széchenyi de Sárvár-Felsővidék (1791-1860), a celebrated Hungarian reformer and political rival to Lajos Kossuth (1802-1894) the Hungarian democrat. The original dedication is removed in the Author's Co-operative reissue.

CONTENTS

CHAPTER I

SATURDAY MARKET

It was a July evening, and the declining rays of the sun beat like red-hot strokes upon Charlotte's Buildings.[1] In the Buildings from six to eight hundred people stewed and panted, at doors and windows, upon beds, chairs and sofas. Some of the children lay asleep on the floor, with their little cheeks pressed to the boards, and their limp, moist hands and feet stretched, palms out, soles uppermost. They had dispensed with every bit of dispensable clothing; the boys had on only tattered shirts and torn breeches, the girls ragged dresses over rags of petticoats, and the babies apologies for shifts, frocks and pinafores. Some of the elder children were out in the court, a piece of ground which stretched from one end of Charlotte's Buildings to the other. A group of small maidens sat there, under the wall of the Mint,[2] rocking their bodies slowly backwards and forwards, fanning themselves with their pinafores, and singing an East End ditty –

---

1   A fictional version of the Katherine Buildings, Cartwright Street, London built for the poorest workers by the East End Dwelling Company (EEDC) and named after the sister of Beatrice Webb (née Potter, 1858-1943), Catherine (Kate) Courtney (née Potter, 1847-1929), wife of M.P. Leonard Courtney (1832-1918). The Buildings, opened in 1885, consisted of 628 individual rooms with shared kitchen and sanitation facilities and were built on land owned by A. G. Crowder after the EEDC was founded to provide an alternative to East End slum dwelling. Samuel Barnett (1855-1913), one of the founders of the EEDC and the vicar of St Jude's, Whitechapel, and his wife Henrietta (1851-1936) had previously worked with Octavia Hill (1838-1912) and sought to apply the same principles of Christian leadership and firm moral guidance at Katherine Buildings they had practiced with Hill. Harkness spent time at Katherine Buildings while Beatrice was working as a rent collector circa 1885-1886 although she did not work there herself. See this chapter, Note 7 below.
2   The Royal Mint. At this time the Mint was located in Little Tower Hill, having moved out of the Tower of London in 1811 into larger premises to accommodate the new steam-powered machinery. The Mint had outgrown the London premises by the mid-twentieth century and with the pressures of minting the new money in preparation for decimalization in 1971 it was relocated to Llantrisant near Cardiff, Wales.

"My Mary Anne
Does the best she can:
Keeps a shop for lollipop,
            My Mary Anne."[3]

A batch of little boys played ball against the washhouses;[4] screamed, fought, and kicked, while the perspiration streamed from their faces and dropped in beads from their foreheads. A batch of bigger boys watched them, smoked the ends of cigars they had picked up in the streets, or twisted strings of spoiled tobacco into cigarettes. Occasionally a mother sallied forth to call in her progeny, to scold a girl or cuff a boy; but the maternal voices were drowsy, and the maternal strokes were languid, owing to the sultry weather.

Charlotte's Buildings were, at that time, about two years old.[5] They had been built by a company of gentlemen to hold casuals.[6] The greater number of the people who lived in them thought that they belonged to a company of ladies.

Why?

"Because they are built cheap and nasty," said the men. "Women don't understand business. Depend upon it, some West End ladies fluked money in them."

"Because ladies collect the rents," said the women. "Men favour men; women favour women."

The outward and visible signs of government were manifest to the tenants in the form of lady-collectors.[7] Several times in the week ladies arrived on

---

3   An unrecorded children's song.
4   The communal areas for washing clothes in Katherine Buildings. Each wash-house had eight coppers (large boilers) for women to ensure family cleanliness and the use was restricted to personal washing, preventing any woman setting up a laundry business in the Buildings.
5   Katherine Buildings were officially opened in June 1885 although tenants were first admitted in March 1885.
6   Those workers without a contract for permanent or long-time employment. For instance, casual dock workers would daily congregate at the dock gates at specified times of the day in the hope of being employed for that day or part of the day. Such employment would offer no security of income and unemployment would be a regular hazard.
7   The employment of women to collect rents was intended to set the tenants an example and thus to improve the lives of tenants in line with middle-class ideals of behaviour. Women such as Beatrice Webb, Ella Pycroft and Margaret Wynne Nevinson (1858-1932) acted as rent collectors in Katherine Buildings. Webb and Pycroft lived in the buildings in rooms 97and 98 between November 1885 and May 1886. Harkness also lived in the Buildings for a time and based her setting for this novel on

the Buildings armed with master-keys, ink-pots, and rent-books. A tap at a door was followed by the intrusion into a room of a neatly-clad female of masculine appearance. If the rent was promptly paid the lady made some gracious remarks, patted the heads of the children and went away. If the rent was not forthcoming the lady took stock of the room (or rooms), and said a few words about the broker.[8] The Buildings were, in fact, under petticoat government, which, like everything else in this world, has its advantages and its disadvantages.

"She takes the bread out of a man's mouth, and spends on one woman what would keep a little family," grumbled a tenant to his neighbour, as the rent collector passed briskly along the balcony.

"I pity her husband," responded the neighbour. "She'll have the stick on him if he comes home a bit boosy."

"Females like 'er don't marry," mumbled a misanthropic old lady.

The Buildings were not beautiful to look upon; they might even have been termed ugly. Their long yellow walls were lined with small windows; upon the rails of their stiff iron balconies hung shirts, blankets and other articles fresh from the wash-tub. Inside their walls brown doors opened into dark stone passages; and narrow winding staircases led from passage to passage up to the roof.

"I suppose rich people think they'll keep us from coming nigh 'em by packing us close like this," said an old Irish woman.

Whatever the rich thought about it the poor liked the Buildings; at any rate, they liked them for a time, just as rich people enjoy hotel life for a season. The children played about the court, the mothers gossiped in the doorways, the men smoked and talked politics on the balconies. Moreover, the rooms were cheaper than ordinary lodgings, and if the tenants were "kept under" by female despots, the despots were kind enough. Many a sick baby was cured, many a girl was sent to service, many a boy was started in life by the ladies who collected the rents. Some tenants grumbled against petticoat government, but others liked it; and all agreed that "an eddicated female" was a phenomenon to be much watched, criticised and talked about.

On the one side the Buildings faced Wright Street, on the other the Mint. Four tall chimneys and a huge reservoir were constantly before the eyes of the tenants. Inside the reservoir rain, hail, snow, fog, thunder, and lightning

---

the observations she made while living there. For further information see 'Katharine Buildings, Cartwright Street,' *St George-in-the-East Church*, http://www.stgite.org. uk/media/katharinebuildings.html, accessed 30 November 2014.

8   Pawnbroker. The rent collector is advising the tenant to find money for rent by pawning possessions.

were made. So said the children. If anyone asked who had taught them these doctrines they answered, "We learned them ourselves." In this reservoir the stars slept, into its depths the sun disappeared, out of it came bits of moons and whole ones. So said the babies. Of course this creed disappeared with babyhood, but like babyhood it faded imperceptibly, no one knew how or when; alphabet and blackboard drove it away, and the schoolboys and schoolgirls smiled contemptuously when they heard it lisped by their little brothers and sisters.

A great many of the tenants were Roman Catholics, so their children went to a school on the other side of the railway-bridge which faces Wright Street. Tiny two-year-old creatures were carried under the bridge and deposited in a big room like a nursery. There they were taught to sing "God Bless the Pope," to answer, "Nicely, thank you, father," when the priest asked his usual question, "Well, babies, how are you?" and to say their prayers with the Sister's rosary. The bigger children were drafted into boys' and girls' schools, when, under the superintendence of Fathers and Sisters they learned to read, write and do arithmetic, to sing by note, so that they might join in the annual service at the Crystal Palace, and to become good Catholics.

By profession the tenants were nearly all "casuals," dock-labourers, Billingsgate porters, hawkers and costermongers.[9] A few superior people were scattered about the Buildings, but casuals occupied the greater number of the rooms; people who had no fixed rate of wages, who made a good deal one day, and next to nothing the day after. The wives of these men added to the family income by charing, tailoring and sack-making, besides doing all the house-work. They were little better than beasts of burden, poor things, for East End husbands have but a low opinion of the weaker sex.

"I'm yer husband, ain't I?" is their invariable answer to any complaint, which means, "I can knock you over if I like."

The July evening of which I speak happened to be a Saturday – the hardest day of all the week for East End wives and mothers. To rise early and

---

9   For an explanation of 'casuals' generally see Note 6 above. In this list, Harkness draws together two different sorts of 'casual' work: those who seek employment by others (dock labourers and Billingsgate porters) and those who earn money by trade (hawkers and costermongers). Billingsgate porters, like the dock labourers, would fight for daily – or part day – employment at Billingsgate Fish Market (formally established in 1699) in Lower Thames Street near London Bridge. Hawkers and cos-termongers would buy goods wholesale for retail; costermongers would have a fixed stall while hawkers were itinerant traders selling their stock (usually foodstuffs) from barrows or trays. The term 'costermonger' would often be applied to both forms of trading and both would be exposed to the vagaries of trade and the availability of wares.

go to bed late was the Saturday rule of women in the Buildings. They must clean their "place," get the children's clothes ready for Sunday, scrub, cook, and bake, whilst boys and girls hung about and husbands did nothing. Little wonder that public-houses enticed them on their way back from market. A glass of something took their thoughts off troubles, drove away headaches, and lifted the cloak of monotonous toil for a few minutes. Alas! one glass was never enough. They began with beer – and ended with spirits.

About six o'clock that evening a girl came out upon the first balcony, waved her hand to the children, and disappeared down the staircase into the street.

"There's Nelly!" cried a chorus of little voices.

"There goes the masher,"[10] said a young man, taking his pipe out of his mouth while he spoke, and craning his neck to watch the girl as she walked quickly along Wright Street.

"'Er mother was a lady's maid," he explained to a new-comer. "That's why she fancies 'erself."

Meanwhile Nelly had reached Abel Street, and stopped to examine herself in a shop window. She wore no hat or bonnet, only a black shawl and a black dress. On her arm she carried a large market basket. She put the basket down for a minute and smoothed the red-brown hair which lay against her low, white forehead. About her face and neck were the blue shadows which usually accompany auburn tresses. These blue shadows are wonderfully pretty to look at. They play about the white skin as sunbeams play about the red-brown hair. They vary in colour from light blue to violet as the hair varies in tint, from the ruddiest gold to palest yellow. They fade when the hair loses its gloss, and disappear altogether when their owner sees the first grey hair in her looking-class. Nelly did not notice the shades or the tints, she was only conscious of a pair of hazel eyes with long black lashes, a nose of no particular shape, and a mouth like her mother's. She smoothed her hair, put her shawl straight, and

---

10 The term 'masher' was usually applied to young men who pressed their (often unwanted) affections upon women. The *OED* defines 'masher' as either 'a man who makes indecent sexual advances towards women, esp. in public places' or a 'fashionable young man of the late Victorian or Edwardian era, *esp*. one fond of the company of women; a dandy'. Although the term is usually applied to the male, Anatoly Liberman, in his *OUP* blogpost 'Erstwhile Slang: "Masher"', notes that 'a woman could occasionally be called a masher'. Harkness's use of the term to describe Nelly, used in the story by a man to describe a woman, alludes both to the effect Nelly has on men (causing them to 'mash on' or fall in love with her) and her consciousness of the effect her beauty has on men. Although here she is 'only conscious' of her eyes, nose and mouth, later 'a long narrow piece of looking-glass' is described as her 'friend and companion'.

hurried along to market.

The people in the streets were enjoying their Saturday "out." Brass bands played at the doors of public-houses; and men danced with their sweethearts. Strains of music came through swinging-doors, sailors performed hornpipes on the thresholds of gin-shops, and the friends of poor Jack[11] lounged against the walls with their arms a-kimbo.

Nelly took no notice of anybody or anything; she looked neither to the right nor the left, but walked quickly towards the market. Her mind was completely occupied by the fact that she was going to buy a new feather for her Sunday hat. Should the feather be red or blue? Blue suited her best, but red looked the smartest. She had but one ambition in dress, that was to wear something "stylish." "To look like a lady," she called it; and the sort of lady she admired was the only lady with whom she had ever come in contact, a friend in a West End place of business. To sit on a sofa, to read a novelette, to sip coffee with a teaspoon, to have someone to put on and take off her boots, was her idea of being a lady. Her friend only did these things on Sunday; a real lady did them every day of the week. To ride in a carriage was to be a *great* lady, Nelly thought. Her ambition did not carry her so far as that. A life of complete idleness, with plenty of smart clothes, and good things to eat, was all the ladyhood Nelly coveted. To mimic this blissful state she strove her uttermost, during the odd minutes she had to spare, and with the few pence she could save from the housekeeping. To-night she would buy a feather to put in her hat; and to-morrow she would spend hours trying to make it look "stylish."

She reached the market, and went first of all to a butcher's shop, where she bought a small bit of beef.[12] Then she purchased some potatoes from a greengrocer, who called out "Buy, buy, buy," in a stentorian voice, when the loitering multitude fingered his goods instead of producing money out of their pockets. Nelly put the meat and the potatoes into her basket, and paused to look at the long tows of trucks covered with fish, meat, and vegetables. She

---

11 Presumably a reference to the novel *Poor Jack* by Frederick Marryat (1792-1848) published in 1840, which tells the story of Thomas Saunders, known as Jack, who grew up an urchin in Fishers Alley, Greenwich. Jack begins his ascent to wealth and respectability as a mudlarker on the Thames, earning money by helping people in and out of the wherries. The friends of poor Jack will be urchins of similar destitution.

12 Nelly's ability to afford meat for the family signifies the relative wealth earned through her work sewing trousers. At the end of the nineteenth century 'families earning 30s. or more ate twice as much meat and drank twice as much milk as those earning less than 18s. But even those earning between 21s. and 30s. could expect to eat reasonably well.' John Benson, *The Working Class in Britain, 1850-1939* (London: I.B. Tauris, 2003), p.97.

counted the money in her little knitted purse, slipped a half-penny into the hand of a blind beggar, and made her way to a stall holding artificial flowers, feathers, ribbons, and lace. A smart young man exhibited these wares, twirled them round and round in his fingers, and advised customers to buy articles upon which he made no profit, which he sold "dirt cheap" for their benefit. Nelly lingered a long time by his stall. She admired everything; but not one of the[13] things was quite what she wanted. In vain the young man gave her the benefit of his advice – told her which was the latest thing out, showed her the sweetest thing in feathers, the cheapest thing in lace, she could not make up her mind, and would not let him make it up for her.

"I'll go to Petticoat Lane[14] to-morrow morning," she said aloud, much to the young man's disgust. "Maybe I'll see there what I want."

With a nod she left him, and turned her steps towards home, only stopping to buy a penny-worth of sticky stuff from an old woman at a corner-shop. She had the Sunday dinner in her basket, and the potatoes made her arm ache; but she walked fast, in spite of the weight, and did not stop until she reached the railway-bridge opposite Wright Street. There she went into a Catholic church, crossed herself, stowed her basket under a seat, and knelt down to tell her beads. Father O'Hara was repeating "Hail, Mary" in the pulpit. His strong voice rose and fell loud enough for the people to hear it, although a barrel-organ was playing a tune out in the street.

"O my little darling, I love you," said the hurdy-gurdy.[15]

"Hail, Mary, full of grace, blessed art thou among women," said the priest, heedless of secular thoughts and noises, intent upon saving his soul, which he found a difficult business. Some priests flee the world, some the flesh, some the devil. Father O'Hara had run away from the demon Unbelief. He had looked into the yawning pit of Doubt, and had turned back shuddering. Since that time he had wrapt his intellect up in a napkin, and on the Day of

---

13 Author's Co-operative Edition: these.

14 An outdoor market in Middlesex Street, Spitalfields, East London trading since the early seventeenth century and which still trades today.

15 Both barrel organs and hurdy-gurdies are crank-powered musical instruments but the hurdy-gurdy is hand-held and the sound is produced by a rosin-covered wheel turning against strings while a barrel organ is a larger instrument and the tune is played by the turning of a barrel covered with metal pins or punched paper holes relating to the valves of the organ. The terms hurdy-gurdy and barrel organ were used interchangeably in the nineteenth and early twentieth centuries. Street musicians would often be looked upon with suspicion because many were foreign and their trade was deemed both a method of begging and a crude form of entertainment. Harkness juxtaposes the church service and the entertainment, bringing together the respectable and the pleasurable forms of working-class leisure.

Judgment he would say to the Deity, "Here is Thy talent. I was afraid to use it."

The church had grown dark by the time Father O'Hara left the pulpit. He stood for a minute before the altar, under the red lamp; there he bent his knee, and gave the benediction. A few minutes later the service was finished, and the congregation went slowly out of church. Nelly took up her basket, and dipped her fingers in the shell of holy water fastened against the wall of the entrance. She held out her hand before she crossed herself, to a lame girl who came down the chancel, carrying a bottle.

"What have you got in that bottle?" she asked, as they walked side by side down the church steps.

"Lourdes water," answered her companion.

"What's that?" inquired Nelly.

"Holy water. Father Gore brought it from Lourdes last week," replied the lame girl.

"Lourdes!" exclaimed Nelly. "Where's that?"

"A long way off, somewhere in France," said the other with a heavy sigh. "Our Blessed Lady cures folks who go there to use the water. It cost twenty pounds to go and come back. Twenty pounds!"

"That's a lot," said Nelly.

By this time the two girls were passing under the railway-bridge, which had no lamp. It was very dark, so Nelly linked her arm in that of her lame friend until they reached Wright Street. Directly they came in sight of the Buildings a crowd of little boys and girls ran to meet them, shouting:—

"'Ulloa, Nelly! What have you got in your basket?"

Nelly sat down upon the first flight of stone steps she came to, and the children crowded round her. She slowly opened the lid of the basket, and showed them the bit of beef.

"Measly," remarked a small girl, looking critically at it. "Fourpence three-farthings the pound."

"'Tain't measly," cried a little boy. "Do yer think Nelly 'ud buy measly meat?"

He squared his fist, but before his wrath could vent itself he caught sight of the sticky stuff in the basket, among the potatoes. He began to execute a sort of war dance, in which the other children joined, while Nelly broke the sweet with a stone. Then she threw it up in the air, whence it fell into a dozen little dirty hands and open mouths; and, with a laugh she ran upstairs to the first balcony, where a door stood half open. Pushing through this door, she came into a room fitted up as a shop. A long board, supported by boxes, ran from one end of the room to the other; and on this stood pots of jam, and jars of treacle, the contents of which were sold at a penny the spoonful. Sugar, pepper, mustard, and other such condiments occupied holes in shelves fastened against the wall nearest the window; and in the window, on a ledge which slanted upwards, were sweets of all sorts and descriptions, toothsome brandy balls, huge peppermints, with appropriate mottoes; green, red, and yellow drops, chocolate, toffee, and new-fangled sugar-plums, which have not been christened yet. A pile of wood lay in one corner of the room; and by it, on a three-legged stool, sat an elderly woman, who was tying it up in bundles. She had a thin, peevish face; she wore an old black silk bonnet, a print body, a stuff skirt, and a large apron. Close to her, in a wooden arm-chair, sat a young man, smoking a short clay pipe. He was of the ordinary East End loafer type; he had a head shaped like a bullet, small round eyes, red hair cropped short, and a thick neck. He wore a bit of red flannel round his neck, fustian trousers, and a shabby brown coat.

"You've been gone long enough," grumbled the woman, as Nelly came into the shop. "My back's nigh breaking a-doing of these sticks. Take the jug, and look sharp."

"Can't Tom fetch the beer to-night?" inquired Nelly, looking as she spoke with some disgust at the young man in the arm-chair.

"Who's to mind the shop if I fetches it?" asked the loafer. "She's too grand a lady for us, ain't she, mother?"

Nelly said not another word. She put down her basket and took up a jug, with which she ran downstairs to the end of Wright Street. There she found a small public-house, where she bought some ale, enough to make the froth run over upon her dress. She returned to the shop, placed the jug beside her mother, threw another glance of disgust at her brother, and went silently into an adjoining room. This was a bedroom. It had in it a bed, a table, a few chairs and a horse-hair sofa. Upon its walls hung funeral cards[16] in small black frames, and pictures of saints in large gilt ones. Opposite the fireplace was a shelf, holding an image of the Virgin Mary, two brass candlesticks and a small

---

16 These could be either the invitations to a funeral or the notification of a death. Victorian mourning was taken very seriously and funeral or memorial cards would often be elaborately engraved, hence the framing of the cards as decorations. The Victorian working classes placed great significance on the trappings of a funeral ('a decent burial' – see Chapter XII, Note 8) and often saved for it by subscription to a funeral or burial club to ensure a 'respectable' interment. The funeral club, like those of the Christmas goose club or dress club, exasperated middle-class philanthropists who would have preferred the workers to save towards unemployment or old age rather than 'frivolous' expenditure.

bottle of holy water. Above the fireplace was Nelly's friend and companion – a long narrow piece of looking-glass.

No sooner was the door between the bedroom and the shop shut than Nelly went to a box and took out her Sunday hat. She put it on, and, standing on tiptoe, looked up at the glass. In the glass's company she soon forgot her visit to the public-house, which had wrinkled her forehead and brought a line between her eyebrows. She became lost in thought. Tomorrow she must buy a feather in Petticoat Lane Market; to-night she must decide whether it should be red or blue. Blue suited her best; but red was so stylish – so very stylish.

CHAPTER II

GEORGE, THE CARETAKER

Next morning Nelly woke up with the pleased consciousness that she was going to Petticoat Lane Market. She sprang out of bed, leaving her mother there to sleep off the effects of Saturday night. She could hear Tom snoring heavily in the shop, where he had a bed under the counter. The canary tried to drown Tom's music from its cage, which hung in the window over her bit of garden – a green box, in which she had planted some musk and other cheap plants between two rows of oyster shells. She gave the canary a weed out of her garden when she had put on her dress; then she began to prepare breakfast. A fire was soon burning in the grate, a kettle shortly afterwards began to sing above it, and, last of all, the table was set with a white cloth, three cups and saucers, a loaf of bread and a half-a-pound of salt butter. It was useless to wait for Tom and her mother to wake up, so she had breakfast by herself, and left the teapot ready for them upon the top of the oven. She put on her hat – the one for which she intended to buy a feather – and went out of the bedroom, through the shop, on to the balcony. The Buildings were very quiet that morning, for the men were nearly all in bed, most of the women had only just begun to get up, and the children were tired after their Saturday half-holiday. Nelly ran along the balcony to the end staircase, and thence downwards. As she reached the gate, George, the caretaker, came out of his house. He had on a light blue shirt, his Sunday trousers and a pair of scarlet braces. His shirt sleeves were turned up, so upon his brawny arms his tattooes were visible. On the right arm he bore a crucifix, on the left a variety of devices from wrist to elbow.

"Where are you going?" he asked Nelly.

"To Petticoat Lane Market."

"Alone?"

"Why, yes."

"Wait a bit and I'll come with you," said George. So saying he went back into the house, whence he presently returned, dressed in a black jacket, a bright blue necktie and a round hat. He found Nelly outside the Buildings on a plot of ground in which bricks and stones lay about, and a board showed that no one had as yet purchased it for a building site. There was a rumour current in the Buildings that the company who had built the Charlotte block meant to buy it and lay it out as a pleasure-ground for casuals. George, the caretaker, however, knew different. He advised the children to make the most of the open space while they had it, which they did, building houses with the stones and bricks, shaping mud pies in the puddles and playing horses from north to south, from east to west of it. Nelly sat on a heap of stones as George came up, and he looked with admiring eyes at her small, neat figure. She scarcely reached his shoulder when they stood side by side, and his hands could meet round her waist, thumbs and little fingers, easy. He liked to see the sun shining on her red-brown hair, and he thought he had never met a pair of eyes like hers, although he had been a great traveller in his time and had seen lots of girls. Nelly ran to meet him, and they walked together down Wright Street, towards Petticoat Lane Market. It was very still everywhere, only church bells and occasional voices broke the stillness as they passed through Orange Street. Nelly examined George's Sunday toilette,[1] looked from his ruddy, good-natured face, his blue eyes and light yellow moustache, to his boots.

"George, did you ever wear gloves?" she asked, as they crossed the Whitechapel Road.

George held up his big red hands, grinning.

"Lor! Nelly," he said, "what rubbish."

"Don't men wear gloves in the Service?"

"Officers do."

"Swells."

"Gentlemen."

"Swells are gentlemen."[2]

"Some are and some ain't."

---

1   Author's Co-operative Edition: toilet.

2   Nelly and George's conversation addresses the concerns of the period surrounding the dismantling of social boundaries: in this instance the boundary separating upper- and middle-class and working-class men, particularly through the working-class adoption of upper-class modes of dress. Judith Walkowitz, differentiates between 'gents' (working-class men displaying 'flamboyant and self-conscious dress, rakishness, and counterfeit status' (*City of Dreadful Delight* (London: Virago, 1992), p.43) and 'swells' (working-class men who place a 'heavy emphasis on masculine display and prowess' (p.44)) both of whom sought to present an external appearance akin to the upper-class gentleman. George's experience in the hierarchical structure of the army has taught him to recognize the difference between 'gentleman' (generally an indicator of class status and wealth, although also based on cultural and social actions and attitudes) and 'swell' whereas Nelly's superficial appreciation of external appearance indicates she cannot differentiate between 'gentleman' and 'gent'.

Just then they reached Petticoat Lane Market, and Nelly's attention was diverted to a Cheap Jack,[3] who stood in a cart, selling a little of everything. George stopped to look at a man who conjured water into any sort of drink you liked at a moment's notice. You could have beer or stout, sherry or port. You paid your penny, and took your choice.

"Won't you try it, Nelly?" he asked; "I'll stand treat."

Nelly pulled him impatiently away, and they walked down the middle of the crowded street, between stalls and barrows, amid jostling salesmen and purchasers. Here a man offered to cure you of any disease or illness by means of his pills and powders; then[4] you could be rigged out complete for ten or twelve shillings; to the right you might furnish your house; to the left eat every luxury of the season, from hot peas to ice pudding, from eel-broth to sauer-kraut.[5]

"What do you want to buy, Nelly?" George asked.

"A feather," answered Nelly.

"Well, here's a shop," said George, drawing up on the pavement before a window which displayed East End hats and bonnets. "What sort of feather do you want?"

"I can't make up my mind if I'll have it red or blue," Nelly told him, feasting her eyes all the time on the hats and bonnets. "Blue suits me best, but red's so stylish. Oh, George, look at that little duck of a bonnet up there in the corner!"

"Have a blue feather," said George; "that's Marine Artillery, red's only Infantry. Have my colour, Nell."[6]

So the point was settled at last, and a few minutes later Nelly tripped out

---

3   *OED*: a travelling hawker who offers bargains, usually putting up his wares at an arbitrary price and then cheapening them gradually.

4   Author's Co-operative Edition: there.

5   The combination of food on sale in the market gives an indication of the multi-cultural social mix of East End London at the *fin de siècle*. Both eels (in jelly or a pie) and hot peas were traditional British London working-class foods: Henry Mayhew claimed that the selling of hot peas in the English streets 'is of great antiquity'. The sale of ice pudding (ice cream) indicates the presence of Italian immigrants, the poorer of whom would earn money by selling ice cream in the street or playing the hurdy-gurdy (see Chapter I, Note 15). The sale of sauerkraut (a pickled cabbage condiment) indicates the presence of German Jews who had settled in Whitechapel and Spitalfields in the eighteenth and early nineteenth centuries.

6   The Royal Marine Artillery unit of the Royal Navy was founded in 1804 and the uniform took the blue of the Royal Regiment of Artillery. George's preference for blue also associates him with the Conservative Party, traditionally represented by the colour blue: George has voted for the Conservative candidate in a recent election.

of the shop, holding a small paper bag between her finger and thumb.

"Let's look in at the Radical Club[7] before we go home," George said, when they left the market. "It's open to wives and sweethearts as well as men."[8]

Nelly shook her head. But George insisted; so she gave way, and followed him up the Whitechapel Road to the place where the Radicals hold their Sunday meetings.

The Radical Club stands beside the Liberal Club, like a twin relation. No love, however, is lost between them. Members of one look down upon members of the other, and call them disparaging names. The Radicals call the Liberals milk-and-water Hartingtons, the Liberals call the Radicals crack-brained Gladstones.[9] George belonged to neither; he only visited the Radical Club sometimes because one of his friends belonged to it, Jack Strange. He had just given his vote to a Conservative candidate who had canvassed the

---

7   Radical in this context refers to the supporters of social reform in the Whig-Liberal branch of British politics. Liberal MPs such as John Bright (1811-1889), Charles Bradlaugh (1833-1891) and David Lloyd George (1863-1945) defined themselves as radical politicians. Victorian Radicals worked to alleviate social suffering without changing the political and economic structures of capitalism. Charles Booth, in *Labour and Life of the People, Volume 1: East London* lists the clubs available to the East End inhabitants in 1889, including proprietary, social and philanthropic clubs as well as the political. There is no listing of any Radical and Liberal clubs situated on the same street; presumably Harkness uses this fiction to emphasize the similar political ideologies despite the supposed political distance between the two.

8   Women in Britain were given the vote on town council and Poor Law Guardians elections in the 1869 Municipal Franchise Act, School Boards in the 1870 Education Act (allowing them to also stand for election at the boards), and County Councils in the 1888 Local Government Act but could not participate in national elections. Although there had been women such as Eliza Sharples (1803-1852) who had been actively involved in radicalism, political clubs were traditionally male-membership clubs. However, this club allows female attendance but only if the woman is associated with and accompanied by a male club member. In this case, George is not a member but attends at the invitation of his friend Jack.

9   Spencer Compton Cavendish (1833-1908), Liberal MP, Marquess of Hartington and eighth duke of Devonshire, became party leader in 1875 when Gladstone retired but ceded to him on his return in 1880 after Hartington had led the Liberal Party to victory in the general election. Hartington was wary of extending the franchise and allowing more democratic freedom in Ireland, opposing Gladstone's Home Rule Bill and declining office when the Liberals under Gladstone were returned to power in 1885 on an Irish Home Rule ticket. Hartington and his supporters defeated Gladstone's bill on 8 June 1886, Gladstone dissolved parliament and Hartington formed the Liberal Unionist group. The two sides of the Liberal Party described by Harkness consider the other either unthinking supporters of Gladstone's Irish Home Rule or a diluted version of Hartington's principled opposition of it.

buildings; for the good reason that a drive to the poll[10] had suited him better than a walk on the day of the election. Which party had "the rights of it" he did not pretend to know; but the Conservatives had the most money, so it was best not to offend them, he used to say.

They reached the club, and found a placard on the railings announcing that Mr. Arthur Grant would deliver an address that morning on "The Future of Radicalism." Jack Strange leant against the wall just inside the room. He laughed when he saw Nelly; and gave her a seat near the little platform, among about a hundred men, but only two women.[11] George sat down behind her, resting his arms on the back of her chair, and talking to Jack about the buildings, upon which, he said, the Company ought to have another caretaker besides himself. It was too much to expect of one man that he should keep order among six hundred people, who, this hot weather, drank more than ever, and slept on the stairs and the balconies – anywhere out of their hot, crowded rooms. Last night he had fetched in the police to stop two women fighting; he had been called up to the top balcony where a man was kicking his wife, and no sooner had he come down than he had found a man stabbing a pal with a knife.

"If I'd had any notion what it was to be out of the Service, I'd never had left it," said George, "not even to please the old lady. Nothing comes up to the Service."

"Not even a wife," remarked Jack to Nelly. But she was looking at the feather in the bag, and took no notice. She was accustomed to hear George talk like that. He was always wishing himself back in the Service.

Presently a door opened upon the platform, and a gentleman came to the table.

"Who's that?" inquired Nelly.

"Mr. Arthur Grant," whispered Jack.

The gentleman began to speak. First he spoke of Radicalism upon the

---

10 Political candidates would offer constituents and potential voters transport to the polls, ostensibly as a public and democratic service as anything else would be deemed bribery, but with the hope that such 'kindness' would be rewarded with a vote. This tactic secured George's vote but his deference to the rich suggests the Conservative Party would have received his vote anyway.

11 See this chapter, Note 8 above. Women were allowed a limited vote at this point and formed their own political groups to support established parties including the Primrose League (1883), the Woman's Liberal Federation (1885), and the Woman's Liberal Unionist Association (1888) but the working together of men and women for the same political ends was not a matter of course. This comment might be read as a statement on the apolitical attitude of women generally or of working-class women specifically.

Continent; the expulsion of the Princes in France, and the increasing number of Socialists in Germany.[12] Afterwards he drew the attention of his audience to the division in the Liberal camp; and said, as the Liberals were so divided, he hoped that the Conservatives would come into office, and give the Radicals time to organise themselves into a strong political party.[13] He then began to point out the dangers which threaten the growth of such an organisation; and dwelt on the fact that a foolish love of glory led to a great deal too much money being spent on the army and navy. He talked of electro-plate Radicals,[14] who rush to reviews, and cheer troops on their way home from campaigns which take bread out of children's mouths and increase taxes.

George began to grow uneasy. He took his arms off Nelly's chair, and muttered that the fellow didn't know what he was talking about.

"Let's go," he whispered to Nelly.

Nelly's eyes, however, were fixed upon Mr. Grant. He was so like George

---

12 Arthur Grant refers to the republican Radicals who gained power in the original-ly pro-royalist Third Republic of France (1870-1914) and forced Emperor (formerly Prince-President until 1852) Louis-Napoléon Bonaparte (1808-1873) and his fam-ily (his wife and their only son) into exile in Britain in 1871. The growing socialist movement in Germany, as well as the French Worker's Party founded in 1880 by Karl Marx's son-in-law Paul Lafargue (1841-1911), was a much more advanced and experienced body of socialists than its British counterpart.

13 The Conservative Party was the main political opposition for the Liberal Party and at this period was led by Robert Arthur Talbot Gascoyne-Cecil, third Marquess of Salisbury (1830-1903) between 1880 and 1894, after the death of Disraeli (1804-80) and was almost as divided over Irish Home Rule as the Liberal Party. The Conser-vative caretaker-government of 1885-86 and the Conservative government of 1886-92 were both conflicted over Irish policy: Salisbury favoured coercion to restrain the rebellious Irish while other members of the party – such as Lord Carnarvon (1831-90), Lord Randolph Churchill (1849-95) and Michael Edward Hicks Beach (1837-1916) – favoured conciliation. This divide was politically awkward because the Conservatives had gained power in 1886 through an alliance with Hartington's Lib-eral Unionists (see Note 9 above). Harkness either set this novel in the recent past or had written it before the defeat of the Liberal government in 1885 without updating the political context as Arthur Grant's wish had been granted by the time the novel was published.

14 Electroplating is an electro-chemical process by which one metal is coated with another, usually coating a cheaper metal base with an expensive metal outer layer. Ar-thur Grant's point here is that the actions of some who present themselves as Radicals are not consistent with their protestations for social reform. Similarly, the juxtaposi-tion of images of feeding poor children and tax reduction feeds into the socialist argument that Radical and Liberal ideology, while professing to act for the workers, favoured the capitalist: state-funded support for the poorest is not compatible with low taxes for the rich.

in appearance, yet so different. He was tall and slight, looked about thirty, and had blue eyes, fair hair and a yellow moustache. He looked at Nelly more than once, perhaps because the place she sat in was conspicuous. When George said, "Let's go," Nelly hesitated; and Jack said to George:—

"Sit down, man. What are you in such a hurry about?"

By this time Mr. Grant was far away from the army and navy, inveighing against people who run after Royalties, who put up bunting directly they hear that a Prince or Princess is going to pass by their house. The expense of our foreign policy and the injustice of our annexations next absorbed his notice, from which topics he returned to England and Ireland, Home Rule[15] and coercion. Last of all he said a few words against English Socialists, and advised his fellow-Radicals to be content with a slice of beef instead of asking for a whole ox.[16]

"Who is he?" inquired Nelly, when the meeting was over, and she was returning home with George and Jack.

"Treasurer of a hospital down here," said Jack. "He belongs to our club, and comes pretty often."

"He's a gentleman," Nelly said slowly.

"Gentleman or no, I don't like him," growled George. "I'm glad I voted

---

15 Home Rule was the campaign by the Irish and their supporters to give Ireland independence from English colonial rule. Ireland had been brought under the rule of the English parliament with the 1800 Act of Union and resistance to the Act took the forms of both physical force, through groups such as the Fenians and the Irish Republican Brotherhood, and constitutional force through the formation of the Irish Home Government Association which, when led by Charles Stewart Parnell (1846-91), became a strong political group in the English parliament and whose supporters were termed Parnellites. A number of Irish Home Rule Bills passed through parliament between 1886 and 1920 until the 1922 Irish Free State Constitution Act gave independence to the southern counties of Ireland (the Republic of Ireland). The northern counties of Ireland remained under the overall rule of Westminster but with some aspects of control through the Northern Ireland Parliament until 1972 and then the intermittent Northern Ireland Assembly from 1973 to the present.

16 This analogy illustrates the ideological differences between Radicalism and socialism. Liberal Radicals aimed to alleviate extreme poverty and suffering through political measures but without changing the framework of either parliament or society as a whole while socialists worked to dismantle social hierarchy so that all would have a stake and a share in the production, leisure and culture of the nation. Where Arthur Grant's ox would be held by the ruling class (the bourgeoisie in Marxist terms) and portioned out to the workers, under socialism the ox would be owned, raised, slaughtered, cooked and eaten by all according to Louis Blanc's phrase incorporated by Marx into his 1875 *Critique of the Gotha Program*: from each according to his ability, to each according to his need.

for a Conservative last week, and not one of those chaps who want to do away with the army and navy."

When they came to the Buildings Nelly ran quickly upstairs, Jack said good morning, and George went to his work. He had all the staircases and the court to sweep. During the week he cleaned rooms out after tenants left, and white-washed walls and ceilings for the benefit of new-comers. He took rents which were not forthcoming when the lady-collectors were on the Buildings, and he kept order day and night. It was a hard place, and badly paid. He did not like it. He was on the look-out to "better himself" – which meant, to find a berth in which he would do more agreeable work and receive higher wages.

When these things were forthcoming he meant to marry Nelly, not before. Until then he was content to "keep company" with her, to take her out for walks, go with her occasionally – very occasionally, for he had to light the lamps at night – to a theatre, and gossip with her on the balcony when his work lay in her direction. He never spoke to her mother or her brother. He did not enter the shop. Nelly was the only one of the family he cared for, and why she was so very unlike the rest was a puzzle he often set himself to find out. He was accustomed to puzzle about things. Life was a puzzle to him. If he had had more education he might perhaps have been able to understand it, but he had never been good at books, and at eighteen he had gone into the army, in which he had seen a great many things and a great many people to puzzle about. After spending twelve years in the Service he had left it, to please his old mother, and had taken this place, because it was the first thing that turned up, not because he liked it.

Directly after he had settled his mother comfortably in the caretaker's house she had died of bronchitis. If it had not been for Nelly, he would have left the Buildings that very same Christmas, but somehow or other he had grown fond of Nelly, and had asked her to be his wife. She was neat in her ways and tidy in her dress, just the wife for a man accustomed to the Service. He wished that he had not left the Service. He hated his present work – cleaning out rooms like pigsties, and covering filthy walls with whitewash.

Besides, he was lonely all by himself. He had had a woman to keep house for him after his mother's death, but she had put things away where he could not find them, and had made such a litter about the place, he could not put up with her. Since she left he had done everything for himself. He had been accustomed to do so in the Service, but it came rather heavy now he had so much other work. He would be glad to have a wife directly he could afford it; that is, as soon as he could "better himself." Until then he must remain single, for he did not wish *his* wife to slave all day like the women in the Buildings.

Besides, children cost such a lot. Sometimes, when he looked at the boys and girls who swarmed in the Court, he felt puzzled. It surely would not be right for a man to have half-a-dozen more mouths to feed than he had money to buy food with; yet, if a man was married, how could he help it?[17] This was the question he asked himself a good many times while he cleaned rooms and splashed whitewash; one for which he could find no answer. But then he was perplexed on many other subjects, especially politics. In the Service he had had no vote; he had been forbidden to marry; his work had been fixed.[18] Now he could do very much as he liked, for the lady-collectors did not interfere with him, and the Company of gentlemen merely paid him his wages. He was his own master for the first time in his life. Well, he meant to "better himself." When he had done that, he would marry Nelly, and see what came of it.

---

17 George struggles to connect the Malthusian principle of over-population with the increasingly political debates around the morality and availability of contraception. Thomas Robert Malthus (1766-1834) published *An Essay on the Principle of Population* in 1798 in which he contrasted the geometric (1, 2, 4, 8, 16...) rise in population with the arithmetic (1, 2, 3, 4, 5...) increase of food production. He argued that population rates were kept in check by 'positive checks' such as deaths through famine, war and disease, and by preventative checks such as late marriage and the 'unnatural' practice of contraception. By the 1870s control over reproduction was being drawn into the arguments for female emancipation but the laws on obscenity limited the discussion: Annie Besant (1847-1933) and Charles Bradlaugh were prosecuted under the 1857 Obscene Publications Act for publishing Charles Knowlton's book on birth control, *The Fruits of Philosophy* in 1877. Although there was a growing understanding about the control of pregnancy, birth control methods were expensive and controversial, which limited control to the wealthier classes who had access to information and contraceptive devices. While George represents the working-class educated with a limited understanding of the Malthusian principles of over-population, he is kept ignorant of the methods of checking working-class birth rates.

18 The Reform Acts of 1867 and 1884 extended the franchise to include men who owned property or paid rent above £10 p.a. Many men were excluded from the franchise under this requirement and because the Army provided accommodation soldiers would not qualify for the vote. The army could not legally prevent George marrying but marriage was generally discouraged on the grounds of inconvenience to the army in housing married men and the consequent restrictions to their mobility. A soldier's marriage would have to be specifically permitted by a commanding officer.

CHAPTER III

MR. ARTHUR GRANT

Two or three weeks later George arranged to have an afternoon out, and invited Jack and Nelly to go with him to the Albert Palace.[1] They took a penny steamer from the Old Swan Pier to Battersea,[2] and when they reached the park they sat down under a tree, on the grass, to drink a bottle of wine Jack had brought from the wine merchant's place of business in which he worked. Nelly produced a bag of cakes and a wine-glass, so they had a picnic. It was a beautiful afternoon. Everything looked fresher than usual, owing to the cool weather; the trees had on bright foliage, and the grass was green, except where the children had worn it short with playing cricket. Up and down the river went pleasure steamers towards Kew or Greenwich,[3] with music on board, flags flying, and passengers dressed in their Sunday clothes. Nelly sat with her back to the tree looking at these things and thinking how pleasant life must be for people who kept perpetual holiday. She had taken off her hat, and the sun played upon her red-brown hair, which looked even prettier than usual. At her feet lay the two men, smoking and talking as they passed the wine-glass.

1 A glass and iron building that had originally been part of the Dublin Exhibition of 1865, similar to the structure used to house the 1851 Great Exhibition. The building was dismantled and brought to London in 1882 and opened to the paying public in 1885. It stood on the Prince of Wales Road (now Drive) in Wandsworth, London, opposite Battersea Park, and held concerts and shows inside while the surrounding gardens hosted displays such as gymnastics and ballooning. The charge to enter the palace affected visitor numbers, particularly as it was situated next to the free Battersea Park, and the building closed in 1888.
2 Old Swan Pier was located on the Thames next to London Bridge. Battersea is a district within the London borough of Wandsworth and the location of the 200-acre Battersea Park, which was opened in 1858. The use of passenger steamers on the Thames had been reduced to pleasure cruises after the railways challenged their general efficiency for travel in the capital.
3 Kew Gardens was founded on private land in the early eighteenth century and adopted as a national botanical garden in 1840 by the Royal Horticultural Society. The 75 acres of gardens were open to the public free of charge and the ornate iron and glass palm house, completed in 1848, was a popular attraction. The 180-acre Greenwich Park, which was also the site of the Royal Observatory and the prime meridian (see Chapter V, Note 12), was first opened to the public in the eighteenth century.

Just then a gentleman came up the path. His hat was tilted a little in front, his open coat showed a white waistcoat. As he passed the little group he put up his eye-glass and Nelly recognised him.

"Jack," she whispered, "it's the gentleman we heard speak at your club, isn't it?"

Jack looked up and saw Mr. Grant, who bowed to Nelly and wished her companions good morning. Instead of passing on, he then stood still, as though waiting for an invitation to join the picnic; and when Jack said, pointing to George, "That's my friend," and with a nod at Nelly, "that's my friend's sweetheart," he sat down on the grass and took out his cigar-case. He offered the men a cigar and began to smoke one himself, but refused the glass of sherry Jack poured out for him, saying that he only drank wine[4] in the evening.

"I saw you at the Radical Club a few Sundays ago," he said the Nelly; "do you take an interest in politics?"

Nelly blushed, and replied that she knew nothing about politics; she had only gone to the club because George went. After that Mr. Grant began to discuss the Irish question[5] with Jack, who was keen on the subject, and with George, who, however, said very little, and looked rather bad tempered.

When the bottle of wine was finished, Jack proposed that they should start for the Albert Palace, and Mr. Grant asked if he might go with them.

He looked at Nelly, as though she ought to give the invitation; Jack, however, answered "Yes" before she could say anything, and they set off. They walked four abreast across the park, but when they came to the garden Mr. Grant fell a little behind with Nelly and let the two others go on in front.

"What is your name?" he asked. "I can't call you Miss Sweetheart, and I don't know what else to say."

"My name is Nelly."

"Nelly what?"

---

4   Sherry is a wine fortified with grape spirit to increase the alcohol content. Jack and George are able to drink a single bottle of wine only after the passing of the 1861 Single Bottle Act, which allowed for the sale of alcohol in single bottles to be consumed off premises. Sherry had been a very popular drink before 1860 but sales had declined by the end of the nineteenth century due to a poor reputation through adulteration, high prices and a fashion for lighter wines during dinner for the middle and upper classes. During the 1880s and 1890s the fashion was for sherry to be drunk during the soup course; Arthur Grant's refusal is based on class habit and etiquette.

5   See Chapter II, Note 15 on Home Rule. George's bad temper is the result of his Conservative politics, which would lead him to support either Salisbury's coercion or Churchill's conciliation of the Irish people, but not the Liberal and Radical policies on Irish self-government.

"Nelly Ambrose."

They had now reached the pond, and Nelly stopped to look at the little boats upon it. She had never been in Battersea Park before, and the bit of water seemed to her a beautiful lake. Some schoolboys were singing a part song as they pushed towards the island; and upon the island swans flapped their wings, and foreign birds walked about, waiting for their supper. Trees and shrubs bent their branches down to the water, and beneath them children played – children in white dresses.

"Isn't it lovely?" Nelly asked Mr. Grant. "It's like a picture in a book, isn't it?"

Mr. Grant was thinking that Nelly looked like a picture herself; one he had seen somewhere, he could not remember exactly where, but he thought in Munich. He was wondering how a face like hers came to be in Whitechapel, and congratulating himself on this confirmation of his Radical opinions, for he believed that with the help of a good tailor, and a little polish, Whitechapel might sit down to dinner in Brook Street.[6]

The pond, with boats, ducks, and screaming infants, seemed to him very commonplace; but this girl, with hazel eyes and long dark lashes, red-brown hair, and slight bending figure, was a picture worth looking at. He began to speculate about her character. He was accustomed to East End girls – his work lay among them – but Nelly was unlike those he had come across in the hospital, the streets, and places of amusement. He looked with increasing interest at George's sweetheart, and tried to recall the name of the picture she resembled, to remember when, and where, he had seen a face like Nelly's.

"I am so glad I met you this afternoon," he said as they left the garden, and walked down the dusty road to the Palace.

"I was wondering what I should do with myself when I saw you three sitting so comfortably on the grass. My wife and children are away, and I cannot join them until I have my holiday."

"I thought that gentlemen did nothing!" exclaimed Nelly.

Mr. Grant laughed, and asked, "Do you work, Miss Ambrose?"

"I machine trousers?" replied Nelly.

"Trousers?"

"Yes, for a sweater in Whitechapel. I can earn a pound a week now I

---

6   Brook Street runs between Hanover and Grosvenor Squares in Mayfair, the most exclusive area of London and a world away from the poverty and slums of Whitechapel. Grant's self-congratulation for practicing his Radical beliefs are based on the same superficiality as Nelly's inability to distinguish between 'gentlemen' and 'swells' (see Chapter II, Note 2); he is only interested in Nelly for her beauty not her character or class position.

machine the buttons; sometimes two-and-twenty shillings."

Before Mr. Grant could make any answer they reached the doors of the Palace, when George took possession of Nelly, and paid for her ticket. The caretaker looked rather cross, but his sulky looks disappeared directly he heard a band playing military music.

He had been to the Palace once or twice before; but it was Nelly's first visit. She was delighted with everything. The diver and the mermaid afforded her the greatest amusement, and when she saw the ballet[7] she declared that she had never seen anything so pretty before, not even in the dancing-halls at Christmas. Mr. Grant led the way to the Café Chantant[8] and ordered tea at a little table, out of doors. As Nelly sat there eating cake, and listening to the music, she felt in Paradise; work and trouble were forgotten in the joys of the present; sweaters and trousers became things of the past; mother and brother were changed into fond relations; her companions were no longer George, Jack, and Mr. Grant, but the handsomest, the best, the kindest men on the face of the earth.

She was rudely awakened from her dream by George, who took out his watch and declared that it was time to go home. He had the lamps to light, and as it was a Saturday night there was sure to be a row, he said, on the Buildings, if he remained away after dark. Nelly's lip quivered, and, seeing it, George told her that she could stay with Jack if she liked, that he would go back alone to Whitechapel. But he evidently did not like it; and poor Nelly, who was always anxious to please everybody, said: "No, thank you."

She rose from the table, and slowly followed George. The spell was broken. Paradise disappeared at the sight of the dusty road, and the real world, with all its hardships and difficulties, resumed its thrall over her senses, its hold upon her thoughts and feelings, as they entered the Park.

Mr. Grant accompanied his East End friends to the pier, talking to Jack Strange as they went about politics. He did not speak to Nelly, but once, when their eyes met, he smiled, as though he understood exactly what she was feeling, and sympathized with her disappointment. Nelly blushed and looked away from him across the river, at the steeple of a church opposite. When

---

7   There was entertainment both inside and outside the Palace, and the General Manager leased specified sites for performance or exhibition. Nelly is as enchanted by the entertainment outside (the exhibition of a diving bell) as the inside (the ballet recital).

8   Literally the 'singing café', this was an outdoor café with popular music and this form of entertainment was prevalent in Britain and France at the end of the nineteenth century. There was also a Café Chanant at Rosherville Gardens at Gravesham, Kent (see Chapter V, Note 17) established during refurbishment in 1903.

George spoke to her she tried to answer him pleasantly, but her thoughts were with some one else. She was fond of George, but he was not the ideal lover she had dreamed about. The ideal lover was tall and slight, had melancholy eyes, and a moustache that curled at the tips, instead of sticking out in straight rough bristles like George's. The ideal lover had long white fingers and a diamond ring, not red hands and arms covered with tattooes from wrist to elbow. His voice was softer than George's; his clothes had a better fit.

Presently the London steamer came to the pier and Nelly stepped on board it, when she had shaken hands with Mr. Grant. She watched him walk away after the boat started, watched him leave the pier, and go along the path by the water towards the Chelsea bridge.[9] She lost sight of him behind some tall trees, but she saw him still in her inner consciousness, saw a tall fair man, with blue eyes and yellow moustache, very like George, yet very different.

Mr. Grant crossed the bridge and went to inquire into the fate of a relation whose election had taken place that morning. The servant showed him a telegram just received from the electioneering agent, from which it appeared that his cousin had come in with a good majority. After he had read the figures he wrote a few lines of congratulation, which he told the man to post; then he took a cab and drove to his club.

Mr. Grant belonged to a Wiltshire family, and was a third or fourth son. He had gone from school into the Indian Civil Service,[10] in which he had done very well, until an attack of jungle fever had sent him home invalided. At the age of thirty he had arrived in his native country to begin life again, and he had brought with him a wife and two children. Now, thirty is an awkward age at which to commence a career in England. Places are all filled in with younger men, nothing is open in the professions, the army and navy are closed; there is little for a man to do unless he has a taste for land agency, or wishes to become a clergyman.[11]

_____

9   Opened in 1858 and built to provide access from Chelsea to Battersea Park, the bridge levied tolls for crossing until 1879. The separation of Nelly and Arthur Grant is both social and geographical, and emphasizes the accessibility of leisure for the wealthy – within walking distance – and its limited convenience for the poor, who needed both time and money for travel to the park.

10 The Civil Service in India was an elite post and candidates were selected for both their intellectual qualities, demonstrated through the entrance examination, and their robust physical health. At this time all senior and important posts would be held by British men who would be responsible for the administration of one of the 250 local districts and, because of the geographical isolation of most districts, would have a great deal of autonomy in the decisions made for the district.

11 The eldest son of a wealthy family would inherit the family property and – if applicable – the family title. Subsequent sons would be expected to support themselves

Mr. Grant looked about him, and decided that a secretaryship was the post for which he was best fitted. It would give him time to write a little, to lecture a little, and enough money to live upon when added to his wife's income. Something better would, he thought, turn up later on. He had prospects. An old uncle in Ireland would probably leave him money; when his wife's father died his income would be doubled.[12] He had political interest; relations and friends in the Liberal party, and a prospective constituency in his native place. He might scrape enough money together by-and-bye to go into Parliament. They wanted men in the House who understood Indian politics. But many men are on the look-out for secretaryships; men who have left the army and navy, Irish landlords who cannot get their rents, men whose time is up in the army and navy, men who have failed in business or broken down in health – all these and others. In vain did Mr. Grant try to become secretary to a member of Parliament, a company, or a club; he was forced to take whatever appointment presented itself. He became treasurer to a hospital for women and children in the East End, where he did a modicum of work for which he received moderate pay.

Mr. Grant had a taste rather than a talent for politics. He enveloped the jargon other people talked in is own phraseology, and thought it original. He had a knack of transposing other people's ideas, not only in politics, but in everything else he talked and wrote about. He was not conscious of doing this himself, and he did not talk or write enough for other people to make him aware of it. He knew a little of everything. He could play a little, paint a little, write a little, and lecture a little. He was a pleasant companion, being good-

---

and their own family through employment. There were a limited number of occupations deemed suitable for a gentleman and these included the army, the law and the Church as well as the civil service. At the age of thirty Arthur Grant is too old to join the army after the Cardwell reforms abolished the purchase of commissions in 1871 and with a family to support he is in no position to re-train for the law or the Church. 12 Arthur Grant looks forward to the death of relatives in both his and his wife's family in order to inherit wealth. Karl Marx argued that inheritance was only the transfer of power over the surplus value produced by workers: 'The right of inheritance is only of social import insofar as it leaves to the heir the power which the deceased wielded *during his lifetime* – viz., the power of transferring to himself, by means of his property, the produce of other people's labor. For instance, land gives the living proprietor the power to transfer to himself, under the name of rent, without any equivalent, the produce of other people's labor. Capital gives him the power to do the same under the name of profit and interest.' Karl Marx, *Report of the Fourth Annual Congress of the International Working Men's Association, held at Basle, in Switzerland*, 1869, *Marxists Internet Archive*, https://www.marxists.org/history/international/iwma/documents/1869/inheritance-report.htm (date accessed 9 February 2015).

natured in small things and only selfish in large ones. His temperament was
artistic, with tendencies in all directions, neither bad nor good, for any length
of time, but capable of being either the one or the other for a limited period.

His wife was a sweet-tempered, phlegmatic woman – a woman whose
children would one day rise up and call her blessed, whose husband called
her virtuous.

During the six years of their married life, Mr. Grant and his wife had
drifted a good deal apart. She rather pitied his variable disposition, and he
had little sympathy with her limited intelligence. He always appealed to her
if people were present; tried to draw her into the conversation, for he did
not like men to think her stupid and women to talk while she remained
silent; but when they were alone they merely interchanged family gossip,
and he read a newspaper while she knitted socks. He was fond of his wife
and devoted to his children. He would not have given up an iota of his
domesticity on any account; sometimes he broke away from it, but he always
came back, feeling sure that his wife would greet him with a smile of motherly
forbearance, forgive him for playing the truant. She was polite to his men
friends, encouraged him to bring them home, spent hours cooking for them,
and afterwards sat by, with folded hands, while he and they discussed what
she called "subjects." If he had a touch of fever she nursed him day and night;
when he was well she let him go his own way without making any comment.
She liked him to dine at his club, if she had only cold mutton at home for
dinner; to spend his evenings out, if the children had whooping-cough.

Such was the man about whom little Nelly Ambrose was thinking as she
lay wide-awake in the Buildings the night after her visit to the Albert Palace.
From her bed she could see a bright star above the Mint, and she loved to
watch it. Her mother and Tom were drinking in the shop, for customers
came in late of a Saturday, and they must while away the time with doing
something. It seemed to Nelly that the Buildings were unusually noisy that
night. She could hear two women using Billingsgate language[13] above her
head, and George remonstrating with them, bidding them to go into their
respective rooms and keep quiet.

Down in the court children played about, boys and girls whose fathers
and mothers would not be home before twelve or one o'clock from the
public-houses.

Nelly knew how it was on the staircases; babies lay there in one another's

---

13   Profane, obscene or offensive language. The porters at Billingsgate Fish Market
were renowned for their robust use of language, as were the women giving rise to the
term 'fishwife', meaning a coarse and abusive woman.

arms fast asleep, with their heads on the stone steps, waiting for their parents to return and unlock their "place." Those tired babies often made Nelly's heart ache. It was terrible to hear them crying at midnight, when their fathers and mothers came home drunk, and gave them cuffs and kicks. Nelly would have liked to spring out of bed and remonstrate with the drunken parents, but that would have done no good; only have made matters worse, for when they were drunk the casuals did not know what they were saying or doing. Men, who at other times were civil and pleasant enough, became like wild beasts the night after they received their wages, and women who worked hard to make husbands comfortable and keep children tidy during the week, grew rough and reckless on Saturday night. George was quite right in saying that the Company ought to employ another caretaker besides himself; that it was too much to expect of one man that he should keep order among six hundred casuals.

"Some day there will be a murder," said George: "then things will be brought before the police-court, and questions will be asked that the Company won't find pleasant."

But the Company did not wish to be extravagant. The Company wished to put money in their pockets; and, so long as the rents were forthcoming, did not care what went on in Charlotte's Buildings.[14]

Nelly heard the men and women fighting and swearing, the children crying, the boys shouting and singing, as she lay on her bed. Above the Mint shone the bright star; she fixed her eyes on it, and her thoughts flew away from the noisy Buildings to a pair of blue eyes that had looked sympathetically into her face that evening, and a voice that was like music when compared with Whitechapel voices. She wondered where Mr. Grant was, and what he was doing.

"Shall I see him again?" she asked herself.

"No," she thought; "it isn't likely."

"He's forgotten me by now," she said, turning restlessly on her pillow, wondering when her mother would come to bed and the Buildings grow quiet; "forgotten me altogether."

So he had. And he would never have thought of her any more, had he not happened to meet her again, and that soon after the first time of meeting.

---

14 This paragraph is removed in the Author's Co-operative edition.

CHAPTER IV

AN EAST-END THEATRE

One evening, about the beginning of August, Nelly went to the sweater's house to take home some trousers. She found the door open; and the form, which ran along the passage, occupied by three or four pale-faced women, waiting for work. She sat down beside them, and undid the piece of calico in which the trousers she had been machining were wrapped. Presently the sweater's wife came down the passage, and beckoned her into a room littered with bits of calico, cloth, and shreds of other materials.

Here, by a table, stood the sweater, in his shirt-sleeves. He was sprinkling water on trousers, and ironing them afterwards. A woman brought him irons from a large fire which burned at one end of the room; and carried them back again. How many times she did that during the day it is impossible to speculate, for the sweater began work at four o'clock in the morning, and worked until eleven or twelve o'clock at night. Consequently his back ached; he had a chronic back-ache. He was a tall man and very thin. His large bony hands showed his joints and knuckles, as though the skin must crack for want of flesh to ease it. His face was lean. His mouth was long and narrow, the lips being drawn out in a straight line above his square jaw-bones. His grey eyes glittered like steel beads; they always looked angry, sometimes they looked ferocious.

The sweater's wife was square, short, and rather stout. She had grey eyes, and nondescript features. The expression of her face was a perfect complement to that of her lord and master. She was what is called, in East End language, "a driving woman." When the sweater went courting he must have thought, "she'll do my business"; and each kiss must have been sweetened by the conviction that she would drive the nail in where he placed it, run it down to the quick without compunction, if it suited her pocket. There was a complacence in her stony eyes that made them even worse to look at than the eyes of her husband; and a suavity in her voice that grated ten times worse than his rasping tones. She could walk into a "hand's" room, and demand why trousers were not finished, without a look at the hand's dying baby; and grind a hand down if food were scarce at home, if hungry children made work a necessity.

The sweater went every morning to a place where trousers were cut out by machinery, and competed with hundreds of other sweaters to do them cheapest; the sweater's wife gave them out to hands[1] at the lowest possible rate of payment, and examined them when they were brought home finished. With spectacles on her nose she twisted round the buttons, looked critically at the stitches, and dragged at the lining; then she haggled about an extra twopence, and ground down hands who could not afford to be independent. She talked about the wickedness of "the poor," as though a gulf were fixed between the people who can afford a butcher's bill and those who can only buy meat once a week in a Saturday market. According to her, hands were all bad; they drank, they pawned trousers, they were idle and good-for-nothing.

"If I had my way I'd put them all in a leaking vessel and send them out to sea," she was wont to say, if anyone asked her opinion of hands in Whitechapel.

In her pocket she kept a thong, which she applied to the backs of her children; and she would have dearly loved to bring that bit of leather down upon the shoulders of her hands had the law not prevented. As it was, her tongue was the only weapon she might use in dealing with them; and this she employed without any stint, stinging hungry women with bitter gibes, and making hands writhe by means of taunts and sneers.

Of all the hands she liked Nelly the best. She was sure to have the work well done if she entrusted it to Nelly Ambrose, and no saucy answer if she happened to be in a bad temper when the girl brought it home. She kept Nelly waiting sometimes, she haggled and scolded; but she gave the girl regular work and good wages. And all this she did because her best hand would have found work elsewhere had she acted differently. So it was "Good evening, Miss Ambrose," when Nelly tripped into the room; and "Good night, Miss Ambrose," when she ran out again. And sometimes the sweater set his thin lips in a fixed grin when Nelly put the trousers down on the table, and wished the girl also, "Good evening."

After Nelly had given in her work and received her money she left the sweater's house and turned her steps homewards. She walked slowly, looking

---

1   A popular synecdoche referring to those who earned their living by manual la-bour: *manus* is Latin for hand (*OED*). Dickens, for instance, refers to the factory workers in *Hard Times* (1854) as 'hands' as Stephen Blackpool is introduced in chapter 10: 'among the multitude of Coketown, generically called 'the Hands,'—a race who would have found more favour with some people, if Providence had seen fit to make them only hands, or, like the lower creatures of the seashore, only hands and stomachs—lived a certain Stephen Blackpool, forty years of age.'

into the shop windows as she went, stopping to listen every now and then to a hurdy-gurdy, or to watch an acrobat performing tricks inside a ring of men, women and children. There was nothing particularly new to look at, but the streets were a change from the Buildings, and the evening air was pleasanter than the stuffy shop and bedroom. All the week she had been hard at work bending over her machine, finishing off long rows of stitches; before she began another week like the last she sorely wanted a little diversion, a little amusement.

As she stood outside a bookseller's shop trying to read the name of a book in a bright blue cover, she heard a voice saying, "Good evening, Miss Ambrose," and looking up she saw Mr. Grant standing on the doorstep.

"What are you doing?" he asked.

She answered, "Nothing."

"Where are you going?"

"Home."

She spoke in rather a disconsolate voice, for she was tired of work, and home meant getting supper ready and washing up. She had had no "outing" since her visit to the Albert Palace, because George had been busy whitewashing the wash-houses and superintending men lay down asphalte in the court. Hands want holidays like other people; they feel the monotony of the "daily round, the common task"[2] quite as much as, if not more than, their richer sisters, and Nelly longed for a little change before she set about a new batch of trousers. Her mind was weary, so weary she took it almost as a matter of course that Mr. Grant should happen to be in the bookseller's shop when she paused to look in at the window, that he should come out before she moved away, recognise her, and wish her good evening. It was two weeks since she had met him in Battersea Park, and she had almost forgotten his existence, although at first she had thought of him all day and dreamt of him all night. She had made up her mind that she would never see him again, and he had faded in her memory, had become mixed up with the ideal, nameless lover who played so great a part in her thoughts and occupied such a prominent place in her feelings. Now she was mentally exhausted, unable to take much interest in him or anyone else unless something happened to rouse

---

2   'The trivial round, the common task' is a line from the hymn New Every Morning is the Love (1822) by John Keble (1792-1866). The full stanza runs 'The trivial round, the common task,/ will furnish all we ought to ask, — /room to deny ourselves, a road/to bring us daily nearer God.' The relentless monotony of work does not 'furnish all we ought to ask' according to socialism; rather, a balance of work, rest and leisure was the goal for a healthy life for all.

her flagging senses, to wake her up.

"Which way are you going?" he asked.

"Back to Wright Street."

She began to move slowly in the direction of home, and he walked beside her, looking down on her tired face and watching her languid movements.

"Have you had another picnic since I met you in Battersea Park?" he inquired.

"No, I have been nowhere," answered Nelly; "I have done nothing."

They were passing a theatre as she spoke. Its doors were wide open, its lamps lit. A West End Company had engaged it for a week, and were drawing a full house. Wives and husbands, young men and maidens were hurrying into it; people with a holiday-look on their faces filled the hall, thronged the staircase.

"Shall we go in?" asked Mr. Grant. "I have nothing to do this evening. Would you like to see what is going on?"

Nelly's eyes danced with delight. She did not answer for half-a-minute. Then she said, hesitatingly, "George wouldn't like it."

Mr. Grant laughed and suggested that it would be time enough to consider George's wishes when she was married.

"Come in to please *me*," he said, "*I* want to see it."

He led the way up the staircase, showed the manager a card, and asked for a private box. Then he took Nelly into a place where heavy red curtains hid her from view when she did not want to watch the stage and the audience, and told her to take off her hat and jacket.

She looked down into the pit, in which she had always sat on previous visits, and felt a "lady" for the first time in her life. Resting her arms on the red velvet cushions she gazed at the people below, thinking that they must notice where she was, and what she was doing; but they were drinking beer and eating three-cornered puffs;[3] they were altogether oblivious. Mr. Grant began to whistle the music, and, hearing him, Nelly became conscious of a strange exhilaration, her feet kept time with the waltz. She looked at him, and quick as lightning came back the thoughts and feelings he had awakened a fortnight before, which for two weeks had lain dormant with the ideal lover.

"So you have done nothing since I saw you last," he said.

---

3   Sweet treats consisting of pastry filled with fruit jam and folded into triangles. These treats are used by Horace Swanky to convey love letters to Miss Didow at Miss Pinkerton's school for young ladies and consumed by the crew of boys at Mrs. Ruggles's tart stand in William Makepeace Thackeray's 'Doctor Birch and His Young Friends' (1849) the third of Thackeray's *The Christmas Books of Mr. M A. Titmarsh*.

"Nothing but work," replied Nelly.

"Poor little thing! how dull you must find it," said Mr. Grant.

The curtain rose. The play commenced. There was French villain, who had nothing French about him but his necktie, a virtuous wife, a man who tried to make love and could not do it, a funny old man, and some stupid young women. When the curtain fell the man who could not make love was being courted by a Frenchwoman, and the Frenchwoman's brother was scheming how he could make his sister a countess.[4]

"Will you have an ice?" inquired Mr. Grant. And before Nelly could answer a waiter had brought her some soapy stuff wrapt in paper, and a bit of paste.

She looked so pretty as she sat there eating it. Her complexion was dazzling by gas-light, and excitement made her eyes sparkle between their long dark lashes. Absolutely unselfconscious, trembling with pleasure, she was a picture worth looking at. Mr. Grant drew his chair close to her, and began to talk of actors and actresses in a way which astonished little East End Nelly. She was overwhelmed with his cleverness and said "Yes, sir," "No, sir," with charming diffidence. What astonished her most was the way in which he laughed at the ladies and gentlemen on the stage; the disparaging manner in which he spoke of this gentleman who spoke so well, and that lady who looked so beautiful. She thought them all such wonderful people; he seemed to think them quite commonplace.

The curtain rose again. The plot thickened. The virtuous wife was forced, to shield the honour of her mother, to become the victim of a secret by reason of which her brother appeared as her lover and was shot by her enraged husband.

"My lover!" she exclaimed, in a tragic voice, which made the house applaud in a way most refreshing to an actress accustomed to a jaded West End audience; "my lover!"

Her noble self-sacrifice was altogether too much for Nelly's feelings. The

---

4   'The rules, or conventions, of melodrama dictated a highly formalized style of acting. ... Points and transitions were common to the acting of both melodramas and classics, and, though actors working under pressure in minor houses, penny-gaffs or booths might lack ... skill and sensibility ... and repeated gestures mechanically or crudely, in principle the technique for expressing passion was the same for all.' George Taylor, *Players and Performances in the Victorian Theatre* (Manchester: Manchester University Press, 1989), p.121. The formulaic genre of melodrama would be familiar to Arthur Grant, a regular theatre-goer, and only the inexperienced Nelly could take such a naïve view of the story being acted out.

little East End maiden hid her face behind the curtain and wept. Scarcely an eye was dry in the pit when the actress came before the lights to kiss her hand; the men shouted, the women wiped their eyes with aprons and pockethandkerchiefs.

Arthur Grant put his arm round Nelly's waist. He could not help it, the red-brown hair looked so wonderfully picturesque with the lamp shining on it, the white neck was so artistic in shape now Nelly's face was hidden in the red velvet cushions. She raised her head and gazed at him, half crying, half laughing, as he told her that things would come right, that the virtuous wife would be reconciled to her husband and live happy ever afterwards, as a reward for her self-sacrifice.

"But the brother is dead," said Nelly, whose mouth was still tremulous. "The others may be happy, but he won't."

"Yes, he will," laughed Mr. Grant. "He will come to life and enjoy a champagne supper, Nelly."

All turned out as Mr. Grant had predicted; the virtuous wife, after having been divorced, disowned by father and mother, starved and robbed of her child, was given back to her sorrowing husband by a strange hocus-pocus of events, in which the funny man played a prominent part. The French villain retired amid the hisses of the audience, and the rest of the company settled their differences in an amicable manner, cheered by the galleries and the pit.

"Your life must be very dull if you can find pleasure in watching a thing like that," said Mr. Grant, as they left the theatre, in which, before they started, he had written a few words of criticism on the piece. (The card he had shown to the manager had had the names of half-a-dozen newspapers on it, and he was obliged to send a notice of the play to a daily in return for the box.) "Very monotonous," he continued, when he had dropped the critique into a letter-box and lighted a cigar. "You ought to have more amusement."

"Sometimes I don't mind work," the girl answered; "but days come when I feel I must see something fresh."

"Do you ever go on the river?" he asked.

"I went once," replied Nelly, thinking of the day George had taken her, in a tub, from the Tower Steps to the Hermitage Stairs.[5] "We mostly go by

---

5   A tub boat was a form of unpowered barge used for carrying cargo and often pulled in trains by a horse or steam power. The steps and stairs were access points from the bank to the water of the Thames. The distance between the Tower steps and the Hermitage stairs was very short and Nelly's experience consists of a ride in a cargo boat from one set of dock-worker's stairs at the Tower of London pier head to another set of worker's stairs at Wapping.

penny boat; little ones[6] cost so much."

"I'll tell you what we will do, if you like," said Mr. Grant. "We will have a row, Nelly. If you come to Kew next Saturday, by the steamer, I will take you out in a boat. I was down there last week and found it awfully dull by myself. Would you like it?"

They were close to Wright Street when he said this, and they stood still while Nelly turned over the suggestion in her mind – wondered what George would think of it. The night air was so cool, so delicious. Mr. Grant's cigar was so different from Whitechapel smoke. Mr. Grant himself was so good, so kind, the little hand thought. She hesitated, then said "Yes" – for her thoughts conjured up a picture in which she saw herself far away from the Buildings and work; out of doors, in the sunshine, enjoying herself. She promised to meet him on the Kew Pier that day week,[7] and to tell George nothing about it."

"I'm sure, sir," she said, shyly, "Mother would be very pleased to see you for A. B. C. in the shop, if you would look in some evening. We are but poor folk, perhaps you'll excuse us."

"A. B. C.," echoed Mr. Grant. "What is that?"

"Ale, bread and cheese," replied Nelly. "We have supper at eight."

"I am afraid, Nelly, I cannot manage it," he said, gravely; "I am so busy."

He wished her "Good night," and she ran swiftly down Wright Street, for she was afraid that she might meet George in the Court. At twelve o'clock the gates of the Buildings were locked, and he often walked up and down, with a pipe, until it was time to close them. But that night he had gone out with Jack Strange, and Nelly did not see him as she ran quickly up the staircase. She found her mother and brother putting up the shutters in the shop when she reached her "place." They did not ask her why she was late. In the East End girls come and go at all hours of the day and night without comment, especially "hands," like Nelly, who help to pay the rent. Her brother grumbled when she brought home less money than usual; her mother accused her of "gadding about"[8] if she had a holiday; otherwise they took little notice of her, and said nothing. They did not care for her much. Tom felt that she was his superior and was jealous. Her mother liked Tom the best. Her mother could perhaps have told why she and Tom were so very different; could have said

---

6   Author's Co-operative Edition: the little ones.

7   A colloquial term meaning a week from the day they made the arrangement.

8   Literally meaning to wander aimlessly but also indicating a carefree attitude, to move around in search of enjoyment. Nelly's family begrudges her leisure time because not working means she is not earning money.

whence she inherited the ways and looks which caused her to be called the Masher[9] of the Buildings. But her mother kept her secret, if she had one to keep. Nelly was only aware that her mother had been a lady's maid before she married a pale, consumptive invalid; an invalid Nelly had called father, until a hearse carried him away from the Buildings, and Tom took his place in the wooden arm-chair and behind the shop-counter, "a year ago come Christmas."[10]

---

9   See Chapter I, Note 10.
10 Probably a reference to a regional term for measuring a lengthy period of time, similar in style to the phrase in this chapter, 'that day week,' which indicated a shorter period of time. See Note 7 above.

CHAPTER V

ON THE RIVER

When Nelly reached Kew the following Saturday afternoon, Mr. Grant stood on the pier in his flannels, ready to receive her. He put her into a boat and rowed her down the river between the fields and the bulrushes. He taught her to steer, which she at first found difficult, and he wondered how it was that this little Whitechapel girl never looked awkward, although shy and rather nervous. Presently she gained confidence, and began to talk of George, her mother and Tom. She told him stories about the lady collectors, gave him quaint descriptions of their ways and doings and described their "followers," as she called the philanthropic gentlemen who conducted the clubs and reading-rooms in the Buildings.[1] It amused Mr. Grant to have an East End opinion on West End manners and customs, especially that of a girl like Nelly, who was so unselfconscious, who spoke without malice, yet said things which sounded malicious. Once or twice he put up his eye-glass, feeling not quite certain that she was in earnest, but the hazel eyes met his with such soft diffidence that he dropped it.

"Would you like to pick some flowers?" he asked, drawing the boat to the side of a field; "there are some about."

She sprang on the bank and he moored the boat. Then he sat down under a tree while she picked daisies.

He felt very well satisfied with himself that evening. He had cause, he thought, for contentment. Not only was he giving a little East End girl great pleasure, but he had just run away from the charms of a married lady, with whom he had been greatly tempted to flirt. He thought complacently of his wife at Margate, the children and the new baby. In two or three weeks he would join his family, eat shrimps and dig in the sand, until it was time to finish his holiday on the Continent. His hands were full of work. He was

---

1   A fictionalized account of the gossip surrounding female rent collector Ella Pycroft and boy's club organizer Maurice Paul, both of whom worked at Katherine Buildings. See Ruth Livesey, 'Space, Class and Gender in East London, 1870-1900', *Women and the Making of Built Space in England, 1870-1950*, ed. Elizabeth Darling and Lesley Whitworth (Aldershot: Ashgate, 2007), pp.87-107; Seth Koven, *Slumming: Sexual and Social Politics in Victorian London* (Princeton: Princeton University Press, 2004), p.193.

translating a book, writing an article on Indian politics, and preparing a set of lectures to be delivered at Christmas. He meant to start a novel when he came back to town, into which he would introduce some curious psychological studies he had come across, and some strange events. He would have no plot in it. Plots had gone out since the time of Thackeray and George Eliot. His novel should be a study of character, that is, an epitome of Arthur Grant.[2]

It was a beautiful evening, just enough breeze to lift the leaves of the trees and drive soft, fleecy clouds onwards, a glorious sunset and perfect silence but for the singing of birds and humming of insects. Nelly, who had picked all the daisies she wanted, sat beside him, framed in dark green leaves and bulrushes. Her long, red-brown hair fell over her shoulders, her hat lay on the ground, her hands were busy tying flowers with grass.[3]

"I know who you are like," exclaimed Mr. Grant; "you are like Pharaoh's daughter when she found Moses; I mean the picture of a girl bending over a cradle with a look of awe on her face and her hair all about.[4] I can't remember

---

2   Grant's novel is anticipating the interiority that would be favoured by modernist authors. He rejects the 'materialist' tendencies that Virginia Woolf (1882-1941) criticizes in the work of H. G. Wells (1866-1946), Arnold Bennett (1867-1931) and John Galsworthy (1867-1933) and aims to focus on the inner life Woolf praises 'several young writers' including James Joyce (1882-1941) for bringing into their work: 'For the moderns 'that', the point of interest, lies very likely in the dark places of psychology.' (Woolf, 'Modern Fiction', in Andrew McNeille ed., *The Essays of Virginia Woolf, Volume 4: 1925-1928*, (London: Hogarth Press, 1984), pp.157-165, p.162.) By taking such a focus Grant intends to concentrate on the individual – and specifically himself – at the expense of the social, communal or collective, so reinforcing his sense of self-importance and the cult of the individual. Reading Grant as representative of Radical politics, his self-interest and selfishness gives the lie to Radical claims of adequately representing the workers in Parliament.

3   Throughout the fiction the descriptions of Nelly, particularly the colour of her hair, have suggested Gabriel Dante Rossetti's (1828-1882) depictions of Jane Morris (1839-1914). Here, as Nelly sits in nature surrounded by greenery, there are echoes of Rossetti's *The Twig* (1865), *Water Willow* (1871) and *Day Dream* (1880).

4   Arthur Grant's description of the image of the Pharaoh's daughter with loose hair might refer to Pedro Américo's *Misés e Jocabed* (1884), where Jocabed is depicted with flowing hair but not looking at the infant Moses; Edwin Longsen Long's (1829-1891) *The Finding of Moses* (1886), where the Pharaoh's daughter is looking at the infant but with dressed hair; or Frederick Goodall's (1822-1904) *The Finding of Moses* (1862) which depicts a slave with long but braided hair bending over the cradle. Earlier paintings of the scene would depict the women with dressed hair and particularly the Pharaoh's daughter whose elaborate hair would depict her status. See for instance Nicholas Poussin (1594-1665) *Pharaoh's Daughter Finds Baby Moses* (1638), Paolo Veronese (1528-1588), *Moses Found* (1570?-1575?) or Orazio Gentileschi (1563-1639) *Moses in the Basket* (early 1630s). Grant's confusion about the painting Nelly

where I have seen it, but that's it."

Nelly laughed. She knew very little Bible history, being a Catholic; but it pleased her to think that she resembled a picture, and she smiled as Mr. Grant spoke of the King's daughter, who had gone down to bathe in the river, and had there discovered a Hebrew baby in a cradle of bulrushes. She was no psychological study, this little Whitechapel girl, only something pretty to look at. She had not much to say for herself; but she put on her wreath and looked like a wood-nymph,[5] while Mr. Grant told her that dog-roses had all been white in Paradise until Eve kissed them, after which they became tinted pink; that a great poet had fallen in love with a little country girl[6] because she had said that, if Adam named the animals, God let Eve christen the flowers and plants, and half-a-dozen other things not worth repeating.

When it grew dusk they went back to Kew. Nelly put her hair up, and sighed to think that the afternoon and evening were over. She could not even take the flowers back to Whitechapel, for her mother and Tom would want to know where they came from; a dozen voices would ask what she had been doing if she walked into the Buildings laden with spoils from the country.

"Never mind," said Mr. Grant; "we will have another day on the river and you shall pick some more flowers, Nelly. Next Saturday we will go somewhere else."

Intrigues with married ladies he knew to be dangerous; he quite forgot that "hands" have hearts.

"I can't think what's come over Nelly," her mother said to Tom, after the girl returned home that evening. "She sits a-doing nothing, and she hasn't been to market."

"Nell, wake up!" said the loafer,[7] walking into the bedroom, in which his

---

resembles might be evidence of Harkness misremembering the picture or that Grant is not as culturally able as either he or Nelly imagine.

5   The reference is too early for John William Waterhouse's (1849-1917) *Hylas and the Nymphs* (1896) so, given Nelly's hair colour and Harkness's or Grant's faulty memory of art, this might be a reference to Anthony Frederick Sandys's (1829-1904) *Perdita* (1866).

6   Presumably a reference to the story of John Milton and his then wife-to-be Mary Powell. The story is related in Mrs [Mary Helen] Meldrum's *A Story of Two Years: or, Gertrude Ellerslie* (Edinburgh: Oliphant, Anderson, & Ferrier, 1882): 'Wasn't it Mary Powell who said to her husband to be, your friend John Milton, that if Adam gave names to the beasts Eve, she thought, must have named the flowers?' (p.37). With thanks to Peter Merchant at Canterbury Christ Church University for this information.

7   'One who spends his time in idleness', *OED*. Specifically, this referred to the able bodied working-class male who is capable of work but refuses to labour. Nelly's

sister sat by her little bit of garden. "Go and get Sunday's dinner before the shops shut."

Nelly did as she was told and went downstairs, dreaming. She heard confused voices in the Court, but she took no notice. Someone spoke to her – George, she thought – she said good evening, and went into Wright Street. She forgot to take her change in the butcher's shop, and bought so many potatoes she could not carry them home. When the children ran to meet her she had nothing to give them; she even spoke peevishly to a little boy who asked why she had not been to market. She went to bed directly she had washed up the plates and dishes and put things straight for Sunday; but when in bed she could not sleep. The star shone brightly above the Mint; she did not care to watch it. She turned restlessly from side to side, and at last she fell asleep, with hot, flushed cheeks and dry lips.

Sunday morning she woke up with a headache, and all that day she stayed at home, refusing to go for a walk with George, saying that she felt tired when the church bell rang for Mass.

In the evening she roused herself and went to see a friend who lived a little further along the balcony. This woman was a kind, motherly sort of creature, and Nelly often ran into her rooms for a chat. She was the wife of a costermonger, an old soldier, with a wooden leg. He drove a good trade in the city, where his barrow stood outside some large warehouses, and was patronized by business men. His wife helped him. At five o'clock on summer mornings the two went to market, and carried thence large baskets of fruit on the barrow to the stand in the city.

The old soldier had his pension, his wife took in washing,[8] besides which they made between two and three pounds a week by their costermongering during the summer months, and from twelve to fifteen shillings in the winter when they sold oranges, nuts and chocolate. They were looked upon as millionaires by the other tenants; and on Saturday night youngsters knocked at their door to say, "Please, mother wants to borrow twopence," "Father wants to know if you can lend him a shilling till next week." They were very good-natured people – in fact, too generous, for their generosity often led them into trouble. They could not help occasionally "treating" a friend,

brother prefers to rely on his sister's income for financial support.

8   The old soldier and his wife are acting against the regulations of Katherine Build-ings, which required the wash houses and coppers to be used only for personal clean-liness and prohibited business use. See Rosemary O'Day, 'Caring or Controlling? The East End of London in the 1880s and 1890s', in *Social Control in Europe: 1800-2000*, ed. Herman Roodenburg (Columbus OH: Ohio State University, 2004), pp.149-166 and Chapter I, Note 5 above.

sometimes inviting a few neighbours into a public-house. When sober they were excellent folk; when drunk they fought, and the old soldier generally had the worst of it, owing to his wooden leg.

The Sunday evening Nelly went to see them they had not recovered from a drinking bout at which they had assisted the previous night. The costermonger lay on a sofa with his head bound up, and beside him sat his wife, who was telling him in maudlin tones that she would never knock him over again, and comforting herself with draughts from a jug that stood beside her on a table.

Seeing them in this state, Nelly would have left the room immediately had she not noticed that their linnet,[9] which had a cage in the window, wanted water. The poor little thing was piping in a thin, thirsty voice that fell on deaf ears, and brains too dull to hear it. Nelly went to fill its class, and while she was doing this she heard firm, heavy footsteps coming down the passage. A knock at the door followed, then Father O'Hara walked into the room and stood silently looking at the drunken man and woman. After a short scrutiny he went to the table and took up the jug.

"What's this?" he demanded.

"Sure, Father, it's only ale for Pat and meself," said the woman, rising up and steadying herself against the sofa.

The priest strode to the open window and emptied the jug out into the road.

"What's this?" he asked, opening the cupboard and bringing out a bottle.

"Jist a drop of something, Father, to raise me spirits."

Father O'Hara dashed the bottle under the fireplace.

"Down on your knees!" he said. "Before our Blessed Lady you shall both of you take the pledge[10] this very minute."

The drunken woman knelt on the floor as she was ordered, and dragged her husband with her. Then, before an image of the Virgin, which stood on a little shelf above the bed, the priest administered to them an oath, and

---

9 A songbird commonly kept caged as a pet by the urban working classes. Its role as family pet was immortalized in the music hall song 'My Old Man (Said Follow The Van)' (1919), written by Fred W. Leigh (1869-1924) and Charles Collins (n.d.) and made famous by Marie Lloyd (1870-1922). As the family packs up their house to make a moonlight flit after falling behind with the rent, the song's narrator is to follow behind the family's belongings to their new lodgings: 'Off went the van wiv me 'ome packed in it,/I followed on wiv me old cock linnet.'

10 Promising to foreswear alcohol forever. The formality of taking or signing a pledge of abstinence echoes that signed by the seven founding members of the Temperance movement in Britain in 1832.

when they rose up he entered their names in a book which he took out of his pocket.

"Now, you have sworn never to touch beer or spirits again," he said, after they had put two crosses to their names[11] with trembling fingers. "If you break your oath you shall both be turned out of the Holy Catholic Church, and when you are dying you shall not receive the blessed Sacraments."

He was gone in another minute, and Nelly followed him, leaving the drunken couple to meditate on what had taken place, to realize that henceforth they must drink nothing but water.

Father O'Hara was Nelly's confessor. She had been thinking all Sunday that she would make her confession before she saw Mr. Grant again, and hear what the priest had to say about her holiday on the river. But as she watched him administer the oath, looked at his stern face and heard his firm voice, she said to herself, "I cannot tell him"; and she went back to her "place," where she sat down by her little bit of garden until it grew dark. When the church bell rang for vespers, her head sank on the box of mould and she murmured:—

"I can't tell him; I can't, I can't."

So the following Saturday she met Mr. Grant on a pier a short way down the river, and he rowed her to Greenwich. The water was rather rough, rough enough to make him glad to lie on the grass when they reached the park. He talked to her about the great telescope[12] on the hill yonder; spoke of stars as suns, like the one she had seen sinking into the west while they were on the river; of stars as worlds, like the one in which she was now feeding deer with biscuits, in which they had just had tea together. He thought it amusing to give her bits of astronomical gossip; to watch her hazel eyes widening beneath their long dark lashes and her face growing perplexed and troubled. She only knew one star, she told him, that was the one above the Mint, opposite the Buildings. He said from her description it must be a planet, and asked if she thought it lived there always. He spoke of the way in which stars move

---

11 Indicating illiteracy in both the old soldier and his wife. A legal signature by the illiterate would be the application of the cross to the relevant document which would be witnessed by the signature of another – in this case the priest. The couple is part of a rapidly dwindling illiterate group in the working class, which by the end of the nineteenth century has been estimated by David Vincent to be as low as 1 per cent. See David Vincent, *Literacy and Popular Culture, 1750-1914* (Cambridge: Cambridge University Press, 1989).

12 The Royal Observatory at Greenwich was founded in 1675 by Charles II and is still the site of the meridian line and Greenwich Mean Time or Universal Time. The 'great' telescope Arthur Grant describes to Nelly had only a 12¾-inch aperture until it was replaced by the Great Equatorial Telescope in 1893 which had a 28-inch lens.

about until[13] she grew nervous, oppressed with vague fears and wondering. She left off feeding the deer and came to sit beside him on the slope under the chestnuts, and presently the stars began to show themselves, dark shadows fell across the grass, the park became quiet.

> "Vraiment
> C'est charmant
> Cette nuit
> Hors du bruit,"[14]

sang Arthur Grant. "Wouldn't it be nice to spend the night here, Nelly, instead of going back to Whitechapel?"

It was very late when she returned home that night. For three weeks she had not been to market, and as she passed through the shop Tom thought fit to remonstrate.

"What do yer stop out till this time o' night for?" he asked. "Things cost a sight more in Abel Street than at the market."

"Wait till you pay for 'em before you speak," replied Nelly, in a sharp voice.

"I can't think what's come over the lass," said Mrs. Ambrose. "She knocks about 'o nights and talks gibberish in 'er sleep fit to frighten a body. To my certain knowledge she only made ten shillins last week by 'er work, and I don't marvel at it, for she's always a-leaving her machine, gadding to the balcony, or lookin' out o' the winder. She's 'ad words with George, I expect."

"A good thing is she 'as," remarked the loafer, who did not like the caretaker, and was loth to see Nelly's money leave the shop. "The airs them two gives theirselves is rediculus."

A week later Nelly came back one afternoon from the sweater's house, laden with work, walking slowly, with her head bent down and her eyes fixed on the ground. As she passed the vacant space opposite the Buildings she looked up for a minute, and there, sitting on a heap of stones, she saw the lame girl who had shown her the Lourdes water some weeks before. On a mound opposite the lame girl sat a little deformed shoeblack, with his chin in his hands and his elbows on his knees. These two "kept company." They had been keeping company for about a year, to the great amusement of the

13 Author's Co-operative Edition: till.
14 Possibly an adapted version of the ensemble aria in *Le Journal d'une grisette* (1848), a French Vaudeville comedy by Eugène Cormon (the pseudonym of Pierre Étienne Piestre, 1810-1903) and Eugène Grangé (the pseudonym of Eugène Pierre Basté, n.d.) It translates as "Truly / It's charming / This night / Beyond the noise."

tenants on the Buildings, who thought it a joke that poor lame Susan should want a husband or hunchbacked Tim a wife.

The two lovers were looking so very disconsolate that Nelly could not help asking them what was the matter. She went through the gate, put her bundle of work down and leant against the railings, waiting for an answer. But neither spoke. Tim looked at Susan, and Susan looked at Tim, without speaking.

"What it is?" asked Nelly.

"Tell 'er, Tim," said the lame girl.

"No, you tell 'er, Susan," said the hunchback.

"Well," said Susan, slowly, "you know as Tim and me've been keeping company this twelvemonth. We wants now to be married, so we goes this afternoon to Father O'Hara and asks 'im to marry us. We rings the bell, and when Father O'Hara comes to us Tim speaks up and tells 'im about 'is bits of savings and the money 'e makes cleaning boots. 'E pulls 'is 'air in front,[15] an' says, 'Seeing, Father, as we're both afflicted-like, we wants to be married.' Father O'Hara looks at us, and says nothing at first; then he tells us, 'Yer mustn't think no more about it. The priest who'd marry yer 'ud merit to be 'orsewhipped.'"

"We mustn't think no more about it," repeated the shoeblack mournfully; "no more – never!"

Nelly looked silently at the lovers – the lame girl, whose crutches lay on the ground before her, and the little hunchback with large black eyes and pale face. Then she asked:—

"Do you love one another very much?"

"I've saved this to buy a weddin' breakfast," answered the shoeblack, taking a shilling out of his pocket and twirling it round on his little finger. "We meant to 'ave cockles and tripe."[16]

"If only we could go to Lourdes," sighed the lame girl, "our Blessed Lady might take pity on us. Father 'Hara 'ud marry us if we weren't so afflicted

15 Tim is tugging his forelock. To pull the hair at the front of the head indicates deference to the person saluted. Tim and Susan's deference is to the representative of a religion that shows no sympathy towards the emotions of its followers.

16 Tripe is a form of offal usually the stomach of a cow but also the stomach of a pig, sheep or ox. Tripe in Britain is traditionally cooked by being boiled in milk and served with onions or vinegar. Cockles are a saltwater mollusc found in abundance on most British coastlines and would be eaten, like tripe, with vinegar. Both of these foodstuffs were generally consumed by the poorest in British society and Tom's ambition to have them at his wedding breakfast suggests the level of poverty under which he and Susan labour, unable to afford anything but the cheapest food for their celebration.

like."

"You don't know what love is," cried Nelly with a weak, hysterical laugh; "you don't know anything about it."

She took up her bundle of work and ran quickly through the gate, so quickly she did not see George, and gave a start when he called out —

"Nell, wait a minute, I want to speak with you."

He had on no coat, and his hat was splashed with whitewash; but a smile lit up his ruddy, good-natured face, and his voice softened when he spoke to Nelly.

"I want you to come with Jack and me to the Rosherville Gardens[17] on Saturday," he said. "It's a long time since we had an outing, but now I ain't so busy."

"Oh, George, I can't come," she answered; "I really can't."

"Why?" inquired the caretaker, looking disappointed. "Why can't you come, Nell?"

The girl burst into a fit of crying.

"What ails you, lass?" asked George, tenderly. "You don't look well, Nelly. Has Tom been bullying you?" he continued, throwing an angry glance up at the shop window. "What's the matter?"

"Nothing, nothing," answered Nelly. "Let me go. I can't come Saturday. Let me go upstairs."

"Well, when will you come?" asked George. "Will you come next week?"

"Yes, if you like," she answered. "Any day next week; which day then don't matter a bit."

She ran away, leaving George with a perplexed look on his face, and when she reached her "place" she flung herself on the bed and sobbed as if her heart would break. Any day next week she would be free to go out with George and Jack, for the Saturdays, the Wednesdays and the other days she had been wont to spend with Mr. Grant would be things of the past. He would be at Margate, and she would have nothing to do but work, work.

---

17 The public gardens in Gravesham, Kent were first opened in 1837 and closed to the public as pleasure gardens in 1913. During the height of its popularity many visitors would travel from London by steamboat to Rosherville Pier. After the sinking of a steamboat named the Princess Alice in 1878 and the rise of rail travel, Rosherville Gardens began to fall out of favour as a leisure destination.

CHAPTER VI

EAST AND WEST

Autumn gave way to winter, and Christmas found Nelly still busy at work. Tom and her mother had no cause to complain now that she took too many holidays, for her machine was scarcely ever silent, and often it was heard until late in the night. The girl bent over the long rows of stitches with pale, tired face, taking no notice of what went on around her, refusing to go anywhere but to church and market. Concerts given on the Buildings by philanthropic West End people did not entice her into the clubrooms, and when a marriage took place between a lady-collector and a "follower" she refused an invitation to the wedding breakfast which Mr. Whitely provided for the tenants. Only once did she appear to take any interest in her fellow-casuals; that was when lame Susan returned from Lourdes. Some rich Catholics (friends of Father Gore) had furnished funds for the pilgrimage, and the lame girl had gone to the South of France in charge of a nun, who, also, had a favour to ask of the Virgin Mary. She had started amid prayers and blessings, with five shillings from the casuals in her pocket, amid bonfires of rags which her neighbours had made on the balconies. Tim had waved his hat as she drove away to the station, and had burnt candles for her in church until she came back. Nelly did not go to see her off, but when she heard that poor Susan had returned no better, if anything rather worse, she left her machine and went to the lame girl's "place," a small cupboard, for which its owner paid eighteenpence a week. She found Susan sitting on a stool in front of a little bit of fire, which she was feeding with cinders. Nelly did not speak, but she put her arms silently around the lame girl's neck.

"Our Blessed Lady didn't wish it," sobbed Susan. "Our Blessed Lady knows best."

That evening Nelly went to church. She looked at the Confessional boxes, and read the names written above the green curtains. Father O'Hara's box stood beneath the station[1] which shows the Christ bending under His Cross.

1   The fourteen Stations of the Cross are depictions of the condemnation and cruci-fixion of Christ which usually line the walls of Catholic churches and cathedrals. The Station above Father O'Hara's confessional box is either Station 2: Christ carries his cross or Station 3: Christ falls the first time. Pregnant Nelly is the sinner for whom Christ died but the image also signifies the pressure of the Catholic church bearing

A little further up the aisle was Father Gore's box. Nelly glanced at that box, but was afraid to enter it, for she always confessed to the stern priest, never to the Father whose gentle face and voice were so welcome on the Buildings. She would have given all she possessed to change her Confessor but she lacked courage to do it. She knelt down before an altar for a few minutes, then she left the church.

On the church steps sat an old Irishwoman, named Bridget, and coming up to them was Father O'Hara.

"Is it Father Gore or yerself?" asked old Bridget, raising her blurred eyes to the priest's face.

"It's myself," answered Father O'Hara. "I'll give you in charge[2] if you don't move on at once."

"Sure and if it's yerself I want nothing with yer," muttered Bridget, rising up and shaking out her ragged petticoats. "Honey," she whispered to Nelly, "give me summat to buy a bit o' bread with, honey."

Nelly dropped a penny into the withered hand the Irishwoman held out towards her, then she went slowly back to the Buildings. She did not confess after that, so on Christmas Day she could not take the Sacrament.[3] She went to Mass, and as she knelt in a corner of the church she saw the lame girl leave the altar with a calm, happy face.

"Our Blessed Lady knows best," Susan said, as the two girls walked home together; "I knows and feels it."

Directly dinner was finished Nelly left her mother and Tom drinking, and went to the caretaker's house. She had to thank George for a Christmas present and Jack for a bottle of wine he had brought her from the wine merchant's office in the city. She found the two men sitting over the fire,

---

down on Nelly, condemning her rather than offering aid as tradition (rather than the Bible) tells of Christ falling under the weight of the Cross as he labours toward Golgotha and being berated by soldiers and onlookers.

2   He will have her arrested. Father O'Hara takes on the role of the police in moving on the poor who have stopped to rest and therefore is aligned with the oppressive forces of the State rather than the sympathy and succor preached but not practiced by the Catholic Church.

3   Confession to a priest is one of the seven sacraments of the Catholic Church (Baptism, Confirmation, Holy Communion/Eucharist, Confession/Penance/Reconciliation, Marriage/Matrimony, Holy Orders, Anointing of the Sick and Extreme Unction or Last Rites). To prepare for the Sacrament of Holy Communion a worshipper must be cleansed of grave or mortal sin through confession and penance to amend for sins. Because Nelly will not confess, she cannot be cleansed and therefore cannot take Holy Communion by receiving Christ's body (the wafer) and blood (wine) into her own body.

and sat down in an armchair with them, while George spun a yarn about Christmases he had spent in "foreign parts."

"Jack," said Nelly, when the caretaker had gone out to light the lamps, "does that gentleman we met in Battersea Park come to your club now?"

"He hasn't been for a long while," answered Jack; "but he's going to give us a lecture after Christmas."

"Where doe he live?" asked Nelly.

"In a road almost opposite the West Kensington Station," Jack answered. "I forget the name of it, but I took him a letter there once from our chairman. Why do you want to know?"

"Oh, I've no reason to ask," replied Nelly, rising out of the chair. "I think I'll go now. Tell George I couldn't wait for him. I have to tidy things and wash up."

She left the house and went slowly back to her place. Inside the Buildings the casuals were eating and drinking, the children decked the furniture with "bits of Christmas," friends and relations shared roast beef and plum pudding.[4] Out in the Court were sounds of music, for some of the tenants played on brass instruments, and others danced. Nelly took no notice of anyone or anything. She shivered as she crept along the balcony, and when she reached her place she drew her beads out of her pocket and kissed her little wooden crucifix.

"I wish I could better myself," said the caretaker, after he returned to the house and found the armchair empty. "Nell's killing herself making them d—— trousers."

"She looks ill and no mistake," answered his friend. "Why don't you marry her out of hand,[5] George?"

The caretaker shook his head and said, as he lit his pipe, "I wish I'd never left the Service."

Christmas was scarcely over when one evening Nelly went out of the

---

4   A traditional British Christmas meal, although roast goose was also very popular during the nineteenth century to the extent that savings clubs (Goose Clubs) were founded to allow working-class families to save towards the buying of a goose at Christmas. The plum pudding was not made with plums but with raisins, and recipes for the pudding can be traced back to the seventeenth century. The cost of meat was relatively high and a Christmas dinner of roast beef would be one of the few times during the year that the inhabitants of Katherine/Charlotte's Buildings would enjoy a meat dinner. See Chapter I, Note 12.

5   At once, immediately, straight off; without premeditation or consideration; suddenly, *OED*. Jack is advising George to marry Nelly without waiting to 'better' himself and thus rejecting the Malthusian prescription of marriage later in life. See Chapter II, Note 17.

Buildings wrapped in a shawl. She walked past the Tower, which stood large and grim in the twilight, through the streets, in which the lamps were already lighted towards the Bank. At the Mansion House Station[6] she took a ticket to West Kensington, and seated herself in a third-class carriage just as the guard gave the signal for the train to start. When she reached her destination it was quite dark, and snow was falling in small crisp flakes. She put her hand up to her forehead as she left the station and looked round her, bewildered. There were very few people about, so if she wanted to ask her way she must go to a shop or walk half a mile in search of a policeman. She walked a little to the right, a little to the left, then she went down a street which slants to the west.[7] As she walked slowly along the pavement she looked in at all the uncovered windows; she peered into the rooms, straining her eyes to see if they had any occupants. Most of the houses had the shutters up or the blinds down, only a few remained open to view. She came to the end of the road, crossed over and walked up it on the other side, halting as before at each uncovered window to continue her scrutiny. Her face was very pale; her hazel eyes looked careworn and anxious.

Suddenly she gave a start, drew in her breath, and stopped short in front of a bow window. She leant her arms on the railings, then put her chin on

---

6   Mansion House Station is not the closest Underground station to Katherine/ Charlotte's Buildings: that would have been Mark Lane, renamed Tower Hill in 1946 until its closure in 1967. Mansion House Station opened in 1871, Mark Lane/Tower Hill station opened in 1884 and both are stations on the Circle and District lines. Although Nelly would travel on the District line to West Kensington Station there is no logical or geographical reason why she should walk past both Mark Lane and Monument stations, which are both on the District line, and is unlikely to be a mistake by Harkness who plotted her geographical settings with great care. More likely the reader is being encouraged to juxtapose the poverty of Nelly with the wealth of the Lord Mayor of London, remember the panicked charity of wealthier London inhabitants after the February 1886 West End Riots – when the Mansion House Relief Fund received a great deal of money for distribution to the poor – and recognize that this charity had made no impact on or improvement in the life of Nelly or the other inhabitants of the Buildings.

7   If we follow Nelly's travels from West Kensington tube station the reader arrives in the attractive area of Gwendwr Road, Edith Road and Gunterstone Road (all of which run generally East to West) where houses, in 2015, sell for up to two million pounds. Arthur Grant's rental of the house would be between 7 and 10 guineas per week (a guinea was worth £1 1 shilling or £1.12 in decimal currency) as opposed to rental costs in the Peabody Housing Trust of 4 shillings and ninepence (57 pence) for two rooms out of average earnings of 9 shillings and fourpence per week for a skilled East End machinist. See *The Dictionary of Victorian London*, http://www.victorian-london.org/finance/money.htm.

her hands, and gazed through the white curtains at a gentleman and two children. The children lay on the hearthrug listening to a book the gentleman was reading; sometimes they asked him questions, sometimes he bent down to show them a picture. Nelly could not see his face, but something in his figure seemed familiar. She leant forward, and into her eyes came a hungry look; while she watched her face grew older.

Then the door of a room was opened and a lady walked in, carrying a baby, which she placed on the gentleman's knee. She laid her hand on his shoulder and stood watching the children with a smile upon her face and her hands folded across her wrapper, which fell in long folds from her neck to her feet and lay behind her on the carpet.

Now Nelly could see the gentleman's face, for the baby dropped a shoe on the hearthrug and he bent down to pick it up.

"It's he," murmured Nelly. "But he never looked at me like that; never."

Her arms shook on the railings; she could hear her teeth chattering; but she remained with her eyes fixed on the gentleman and the baby. She was wondering about his changed expression, dumbly feeling that it had something to do with the little child he held on his knee, whose tiny hand was clasped round the ring he wore on his finger. She paid no attention to the other children, she scarcely looked at their mother, but she gazed at the gentleman and the baby. With large round eyes and clenched hands she watched every movement of the baby's arms and legs as it clutched at the gentleman's eye-glass; marked every kiss its father gave it, every look that passed over its father's face, as he sat there with his arm round it in the semi-light, semi-darkness.

"He never looked at me like that," murmured Nelly, drawing back behind a stone pillar near the steps, "never."

Standing behind the pillar, she did not notice Mr. Grant give the child to its mother and come to the window. Had she seen him there, looking out at the night, thinking whether he would go to his club or see what his wife had at home for dinner, saying to himself that it was a nuisance to be poor and forced to live in the suburbs, yawning, and putting up his eye-glass, she would have been astonished. Whitechapel knows nothing of metempsychosis;[8] it is

---

8 'Transmigration of the soul, passage of the soul from one body to another; *esp.* (chiefly in Pythagoreanism and certain Eastern religions) the transmigration of the soul of a human being or animal at or after death into a new body of the same or a different species' *OED*. Harkness is using the term to suggest the impossibility of empathy between classes: Nelly (and 'Whitechapel' generally) could not 'inhabit' the bodies or minds of the middle and upper classes; they would be unable to understand the *ennui* of Mr. Grant, in his warm home, surrounded by his family with worries

the land of dumb thought and dumb feeling, unless it visits the gin shop and takes to dram drinking.

The next time Nelly looked at the window she found the shutters closed and the picture she had been watching vanished into darkness. Slowly, very slowly, she left the spot, and walked back to the station. As she went she seemed to see Mr. Grant's face bending over the baby. His changed expression perplexed her; she could not understand it. But she felt that he lived in a different world from the one she had imagined – a world shut in by the golden gates of domestic peace and happiness. This was the man she had seen in the parks, and on the river; only then he had looked as men look at "sweethearts," not as men look at babies.

When she drew near the station she put her hand into her pocket to find her return ticket. To her surprise her pocket was empty. In vain she searched the road and the pavement, her purse was gone – gone altogether. Either she had dropped it or it had been stolen; there was no trace of it left, although she turned her pocket inside out, and shook her dress. A forlorn, forsaken feeling came over Nelly. She sat down on a doorstep, and sitting there she felt how far, how very far the East is from the West. She realized that Whitechapel may talk to Kensington, and Kensington may shake hands with Whitechapel, but between them there is a great gulf fixed, the thought of which made her head ache and her heart sink.

At last she rose up and gazed about her, vaguely wondering how she should get back to the Buildings. It was a long way to walk, and she did not know in which direction she ought to begin walking. The roads looked all alike; the rows of houses showed no difference. Snow was falling fast; and as she stood there, with the snowflakes beating upon her face, she heard a church bell strike nine. She felt tired, and very cold. Her body shook, her legs were unsteady in their movements. She could not spend the night in the streets; she must go home, and she must go home on foot because she had no money to pay for train or omnibus.

She went slowly and painfully past the railway station, and when she came to some steps she asked a man the way to the Bank. He stared at her, and, seeing her stagger, turned on his heel. She did not ask again, but went straight on in one direction. Sometimes people jostled against her, boys almost knocked her over, but she stumbled forwards, and came at last to a place where some omnibuses were waiting outside a tavern. "Bank" was written on the door of one omnibus, and she looked with longing eyes at the red seats inside it. She was so very weary. She leant against a wall opposite

---

about food that concerned only variety and not scarcity.

the omnibus and wondered how she could possibly get back to Whitechapel.

"I can't walk one step further," she said to herself. "If I can't ride home I must lie down in the street, put my head somewhere, and go to sleep."

While she was wondering what would become of her a young man passed by. His face was marked with lines of work; its expression was very earnest, very benevolent. He looked at Nelly; and she, not knowing what gave her courage to speak, said: —

"Oh, sir, I've lost my purse. Won't you lend me twopence?"

The young man put his hand into his pocket, but before he could answer a policeman came up.

"Move on," said the policeman roughly, to Nelly.

"Leave the girl alone!" exclaimed the young man.

"I've nothing to do with you, sir," said the policeman; "but this young woman —— "

"Has lost her purse," interrupted the young man. "Will you have a cab, or go by the omnibus?" he asked, turning to Nelly.

"I only want twopence," faltered Nelly. "I'll send it back. But I am so tired, sir; so tired."

"She's drunk," muttered the policeman.

"Let me lend you five shillings,"[9] said the young man. "You won't? Well, here is an omnibus."

He helped her into a seat, paid the conductor her fare, and wished her a pleasant "good night." As he walked away he raised his hat. That young man is well known in London; his name is fast becoming famous; but, surely, if our actions were measured by their real worth, not as they are talked about, his kindness to Nelly would be reckoned of greater value than all his pleadings in Court – than all his future eminence!

9   Sixty pence in decimal money and more than half of what Nelly would earn in a week at her sewing machine. See this chapter, Note 7 above.

CHAPTER VII

A CAPTAIN IN THE SALVATION ARMY

Winter was over, and spring was making its first appearance, when Nelly went one day to the sweater's house with a bundle of trousers. She walked slowly, for she knew that the work ought to have been carried home some days previously, that the sweater's wife would be cross. Besides, she was tired and the distance seemed long, longer than it used to be last year! Last year! "Ah!" wondered Nelly, "when was that?" She rested on doorsteps as she went, and put her bundle down every five or ten minutes. Her dress was draggled, the feather in her hat was limp; evidently she had not lately seen much of her friend in the looking-glass.

When she came to the house she found the sweater's wife in the passage scolding the maid-servant. It is a curious fact that people who only keep one servant generally find in her more faults, if not vices, than are found by mistresses of large households in ten or twelve domestics. The sweater's wife never kept a servant more than a month, for sometimes the servant ran away, and invariably the servant gave notice within four weeks. Servants were all bad in Whitechapel, said the sweater's wife, and no country servant would live in such a wicked neighbourhood; so her voice was generally heard scolding in the kitchen, when it was not scolding in the workshop. Nelly could not have arrived at a more unfortunate moment, for the sweater's wife had worked herself into a state of excitement in which she longed to have some just cause for wrath. Her children were all at school, so she could not bring the thong out of her pocket, and the maid-servant had retired weeping into the kitchen as Nelly, tired and exhausted, came up the stone steps.

The girl sat down on a form in the passage and began to count the trousers she had stitched during the week. She knew that it was useless to make excuses for bringing the work home late, so she waited for the sweater's wife to speak. But the sweater's wife remained silent. Nelly looked up, and something in the woman's face made her turn pale. Her head sank down, she covered her face with her hands, and the trousers fell on the ground at her feet.

Then the sweater's wife gave vent to her feelings. She called Nelly by the most terrible names that have ever been invented, no term in the feminine vocabulary seemed to her bad enough for the poor "hand" who trembled before her. There is nothing in this world so hard, so cold, as a woman who prides herself upon being virtuous; no one so barren of comfort as a wife who has had no temptation to leave the path of righteousness. Poor little trembling Nelly only half understood the paragon's speech, but she felt as though she were being thrust down, down into a pit, the bottom of which she could never reach, into which she must sink, alone, helpless. At last she rose up and crept through the open door, into the street, having heard that only "honest" women should make trousers for virtuous sweaters, not girls like Nelly Ambrose.

"Where shall I go?" she wondered. "What shall I do?"

She sat down on a doorstep to think. They would not care to have her at home unless she had work, she said to herself. In her life work meant mother, brother, food, rent. She had forgotten to wait for her money; she had left the trousers in the passage, and come away without it. She could not make up her mind to go back; yet she was afraid to meet Tom penniless. She went a little way towards the sweater's house – then she stopped.

"No," she thought. "I will face Tom sooner than that dreadful woman. I will try to get work somewhere else. I will do anything."

She knew other sweaters; so she started off to inquire where a hand was wanted. Necessity made her walk fast, and she hurried along, although hungry and weary, determined to find employment. Alas! each sweater told her that he had no need of her services; times were bad, work was slack, she might be wanted later on, but not at present. She looked in at the shop windows, hoping to see cards saying that hands were wanted, but no cards were hung up. Last year she had seen numbers of such notices; she had felt so independent; now she grew every minute more hopeless, more desperate.

The spring afternoon changed into chilly evening, and still she wandered on, afraid to go back to the Buildings, trembling at the thought of telling Tom and her mother that she was "out of work." Once it flashed into her mind that she had better make her way to the priest's house and let Father O'Hara know all about it; but she had not sufficient courage to go there, she was afraid of the tall, stern priest, who looked as though sin were a thing to be trampled upon rather than pitied, whose voice frightened penitents into hiding instead of confessing faults.

Father O'Hara lived in an atmosphere of doctrine and ritual, scourging himself free from intellectual weakness. He had little sympathy with sinful flesh; he thought it ought to be scourged into holiness. The death of a saint was pleasing in God's sight, for the Deity rejoiced in witnessing pain borne for His sake; the death of a sinner satisfied His righteousness. Such was Father

O'Hara's faith, and he clung to it, knowing that it would slip from his grasp unless he blinded his intellect, held it fast.

At last Nelly went back to the Buildings. It was growing dark when she reached the shop, so she did not notice her mother and Tom talking together in the window; see the looks they threw at her as she passed into the bedroom. But presently the bedroom door opened, and the loafer came in. Directly the girl saw him she gave a wild piercing shriek, for in his hand he held a stick. She cowered, and called aloud on the Virgin Mary, while the bully advanced towards her. Shriek followed shriek. Then Nelly rushed wildly out of the room, past her mother, into the street.

She ran into the vacant space opposite the Buildings, with her red-brown hair streaming behind her, and her eyes full of terror and anguish. There, in a corner, she lay down on the ground – alone at last. No one came to disturb her; she was left to herself, in cold, hunger, and darkness. Bruised in body and wounded in spirit, with visions of sweaters' wives and bullying brothers, she shivered and wept; while Tom enjoyed the consciousness of having done his duty, and her mother drank.

She fell asleep, with her head on a heap of stones and bricks, and there she slept until the caretaker came to look for her. He had heard strange tales on the Buildings (in them gossip travels fast). He had been told that the sweater's wife had paid Nelly's mother a visit, and that Tom had, in consequence, turned his sister out into the street. He could not believe it: but a little boy had said that at nine o'clock Nelly had been seen flying into the vacant space, that she had not come back, but lay there still, quite quiet, "all of a heap." The caretaker then took a lantern and went to look for his sweetheart. He was still incredulous, and yet – and yet?

He found Nelly stretched on the ground, with her red-brown hair across her pale face and her eyes shut. As he bent over her the light of the lantern woke her up. She started, looked at him, pushed her hair back, and turned on her elbow. George thought that he had never seen her look so beautiful as she did that night.

"Nell, lass," he said, "it isn't true, is it?"

Into her hazel eyes came a look like that you see in the eyes of an animal caught in a trap.

"Nell, tell me it isn't true," George said. "Just say it isn't true, Nelly."

She made no answer, and he let the light fall full on her face. He did not speak for some minutes. He stood silently thinking. Then he said: —

"Follow me, Nelly. You can't stay out here all night."

She rose up and walked by his side out of the vacant space into Wright

Street. Very few people were about, and those who saw her were afraid to make any remark, for the caretaker was feared as well as liked on the Buildings. He blew out the light and left the lantern on his door-step; afterwards he walked slowly in the direction of the Aldgate Station, followed by Nelly. The girl plaited her hair as they went, and tried to put her dress straight. George could hear her sobbing, but he walked on without looking at her, taking no notice. They reached a small street leading towards Bishopsgate,[1] and there he knocked at a door. When it was opened he asked for Captain Lobe,[2] and hearing that the Captain was upstairs he mounted a staircase and knocked again.

"Come in!" shouted a voice inside a room.

They went in. There, sitting on a table, with his arms crossed and his legs hanging down, was a little fellow in uniform. He had an "S" on his collar, otherwise he might have been taken for a Volunteer Captain. There was a smartness about him which spoke of the army; he was neat from his short-cropped hair to his boots — so spick and span, no corps need have been ashamed to own him. He looked eighteen, but was older most likely, for his eyes had a wider range of sympathies than those of boys have, and his voice was the voice of a man.

By a fire stood an elderly woman. She was making tea, and as George and Nelly came in she held out a cup to the little Salvation Captain.[3] Her face was careworn, but placid and contented.

The two were alone in the room but evidently other people were expected, for chairs stood by the fire, and half-a-dozen cups and saucers were on the

---

1   See Note 5 on the Rescue Lassie's Rooms below.

2   This character is the protagonist of Harkness's third novel, originally serialized in the *British Weekly: A Journal of Social and Christian Progress* between 6 April and 14 December 1888, entitled *Captain Lobe: a Story of the Salvation Army* and republished in 1891 under the title *In Darkest London*. Harkness's multiple uses of the Captain, and the 'penny gaff' in this area which appears in both *Out of Work* and *In Darkest London*, creates a sense of community across the first three books and presents a continuing need for change and improvement in the lives of the poor from three different perspectives.

3   William Booth (1829-1912) and his wife Catherine (1829-1890) founded the Salvation Army in Whitechapel in 1865. The institution was originally known as the Christian Mission but became the Salvation Army in 1878, a change of name suggested by the Booth's son, William Bramwell Booth (1856-1929). The change also brought a hierarchy based on military rankings and the adoption of a Salvation Army uniform. The rankings mirrored those of the national army, was headed by 'General' Booth and populated with soldiers (members aged over 14) as well as the ranks Sergeant, Envoy, Cadet, Lieutenant, Captain, Major, Lieutenant-Colonel, Colonel and Commissioner. A member achieves Captain status after five years' service.

table. In the fender was a plate of buttered toast, and by the side of the grate puffed a large black kettle. The room was barely furnished; it had no carpet, no table-cloth; in fact, no ornament of any sort except a large placard nailed against the wall, which stated: —

"In wet weather all female officers are ordered to wear goloshes."[4]

Directly the little Captain saw George and Nelly he sprang down from the table and went to meet them, asking: —

"What can I do for you?"

Then, without waiting for an answer, he pointed to a chair, and said to Nelly: —

"Sit down; the sergeant will give you some tea. How cold and tired you look, lassie."

His voice was strangely gentle and sympathetic. You do not often hear a voice like it, either in the East or the West End of London; but then there is in this world only one such little Salvation Captain. In another minute he was back on the table swinging his legs, while the sergeant poured out a cup of tea for Nelly and he took up the buttered toast from the grate, hoping that the girl would eat some of it.

Nelly sank down on the chair the Captain pointed out to her, and leant her head against the wall. She tried to thank the sergeant for the tea, but could not manage to make her voice audible. She shook her head at the toast. She stopped sobbing, but tears fell on her knee; her hands trembled so much she would have dropped the teacup had not the little Captain jumped off the table in time to catch it.

"I'll get you some brandy," he said, going to a cupboard. "Sergeant, give me a glass."

Meanwhile George looked on, twirling his hat in his fingers, without speaking. He refused to sit down, and would not take tea or toast. He waited until Nelly had finished the brandy, then he was about to say something, when the door opened, and two girls, with shawls on their heads, came into the room. They wished the Captain and the sergeant good evening, and sat down by the fire to drink tea, while the elderly woman made inquiries about the weather, and asked if they had on dry boots.

"Whose beat are you on to-night?" inquired the Captain.

They answered, "X.'s"

"O, that's all right; but don't be late," said the Captain. "Sergeant Grey

---

4   Galoshes originally referred to a shoe with a wooden sole but in this context the reference is to an overshoe (now usually made of India rubber) worn to protect the ordinary shoe from wet or dirt, *OED*.

always gets nervous if you are out later than usual, even if X. is on duty. Good night, lassies!"

After the girls went away George took the Captain aside and they had a long talk, in which the sergeant joined them, at the Captain's request. Nelly sat by, with her eyes shut, enjoying a sense of peace and comfort which she had not experienced for nearly a twelvemonth. The room felt so warm after the cold, dreary streets; the people in it had voices so unlike those of Tom and the sweater's wife. Her only fear was that all this warmth and kindness would suddenly vanish. Then, what would become of her? Who would give her a place to lie down in? All she wanted was to lie down and be quiet.

"Nelly," said George, coming up to the fireplace, "would you like to go home with the sergeant? She has a room to let."

"Oh, George," sobbed the girl, "I'm out of work."

"I know that," the caretaker answered. "I'll pay for it."

"How can you find the money?"

"I shall take it out of the post-office."

"The post-office!"

"Why, yes," said George, slowly. "I've been saving money to furnish a house directly I could better myself; I'll take that."

He turned away, and as he left the room with the Captain, Nelly heard him mutter, "I wish I'd never left the Service."

Directly the two men departed the sergeant cleared the table, raked the fire out of the grate, and told Nelly that she was ready to go home. "Mine's a poor place," she said, "but nice and quiet. I work all day and only help the Army of an evening, so you mustn't mind the fire being out when we get back. I'll give you some supper, lassie; then you shall go to bed. You look almost worn out."

It was not far from the Rescue Lassies' Room[5] to the sergeant's place, only about five minutes' walk, and Nelly did not find the way long, for the motherly woman gave the girl an arm to lean on and talked to her all the time about household matters, how they should manage with the oven, who should use the copper first on washing days, the cheapest grocer and the best milkshop. When they reached the house she took Nelly downstairs into a

---

5   Elizabeth Cottrill (n.d.), a Salvation Army member in Whitechapel, began the rescue operation by taking converted girls from the streets into her own home. Florence Booth (1861-1957), wife of Bramwell Booth, managed the Salvation Army's women's social and rescue work from 1882. In 1884 the Salvation Army opened its first rescue home in Hanbury Street, Whitechapel. Hanbury Street runs from Vallance Gardens westward towards Bishopsgate and is, presumably, the place of Nelly's rescue.

little kitchen, hung her bonnet on a nail, and cooked the supper. George had, she said, arranged everything; Nelly was not to trouble about payment.

"You mustn't cry, lassie," she told the girl. "Cheer up. I'll get your room ready and you shall go to bed at once."

Nelly could scarcely believe that it was not all a dream, that she would not awake and find herself back in the noisy Buildings. She looked at the neat little kitchen, with its whitewashed walls and red brick floor; she stroked the cat that purred as it rubbed its back against her dress; she watched the sergeant bustling about with sheets and blankets, and wondered how she came to be sitting there instead of with Tom and her mother in the shop.

"You're at home now, lassie," said the sergeant as she wished Nelly good night. "You belong to us."

CHAPTER VIII

WHO IS IT?

The following evening George paid the little Salvation Captain a visit. He lived in lodgings near the barracks, and when the caretaker came into his room he was lying curled up on an old sofa, studying some rules just issued by the General.[1] There was one thing about him which all must have noticed; namely, he never sat in the same position for two consecutive minutes. The position he liked best was one on the table, where he could swing his legs, but if he was obliged to be in a chair he twisted himself into the oddest shapes. He threw his arms round the back of the seat; he sat now on one leg, and now on the other; he crossed his knees, he drew in his feet, he contorted his body, he *could* not keep quiet for more than one minute. When George knocked at the door he had just finished his tea. The remains of it were on the table – all except the eggshells, which he had pitched into the grate. He was not in uniform. He had on an old jacket frayed at the neck and wrists, some very old trousers, and slippers bought in Whitechapel for eighteenpence. The large bare room he sat in looked out on the Whitechapel Road – that road, so full of interest, which fascinates people who watch it more than any other thoroughfare in London. He was too busy to spend much time in looking at it, but sometimes he put his head out of the window to lament over the sinners he consigned to the burning pit, to offer up a prayer for Whitechapel.

George wished the Captain good evening, and sat down. He took a good-sized envelope out of his pocket and slowly spread its contents on the table, smoothing the papers as he laid the one above the other before him.

The little Captain sprang into his favourite position and sat swinging his legs, wondering what was going to happen.

"This," George told the Captain, putting his finger on a letter with a large monogram, "is from the colonel."[2]

"These," he continued pointing to other letters are from the officers who had me as servant."

"And that," he said, looking proudly at a bit of parchment, "is my

---

1   William Booth. See Chapter VII, Note 3.

2   Not to be confused with the Salvation Army rankings; George is referring to the chain of command in his previous position, the Marine Artillery.

character when I left the Service. Eight years and twenty-three days on water, the rest on land – twelve years' character altogether. I've kept it as it is, because I couldn't be taking in and out of a frame while I was trying to better myself; but I meant to have it framed when I married – framed and hung up."

Then George laid his head down on the table and cried like an infant.

The little Captain slung his arm round the caretaker's neck and sat looking at the big man beside him in silence. His eyes rested on the characters, especially upon the bit of parchment of which George so proud. At last he said: —

"You won't give her up?"

"Would YOU marry her now?" asked the caretaker.

"Oh, I'm different," answered the little Captain. "The General doesn't set his face against marriages, but he's very particular. Names have to be sent in to headquarters before officers get married, and they can only marry if the General gives his consent. If I wanted to marry a girl like your sweetheart I doubt if he'd let me do it. But you're different."

"I mightn't marry while I was in the Service," said George. "I wish I'd never left it. There's nothing like the Service."

"I can't say how it would have been with me for certain," continued the little Captain, thoughtfully. "The General sets his face against jilts. If a man gets a woman to care for him, or a woman lets a man think she loves him and nothing comes of it, there's a court martial. Jilts are turned out of the Army. You see the Army preaches dead against jilting."

"It's so rum to hear you talking of the Army," said George, looking up at the little fellow. "To hear you talk, one would think yours was a real Service."

"So it is, isn't it?"

"What! With women in it!"

"I don't know how we'd do without them," said the Captain. "Women have a way of putting things that men haven't. For the matter of that, I've seen the biggest sinners brought home by the littlest saints. The General sets great store on women, I can tell you. He thinks no end of them and their work. They over-do it sometimes, make themselves ill and nervous; but the devil would have a lot more people to fill his place if it weren't for women in the Army."

"Well, I'm all for women keeping quiet myself," said the caretaker. "I don't like to hear them preaching and singing in the streets; but that's my taste, and if others think different I've nothing to say against it. Do you know why I came to you last night?"

"No."

"I heard of you from the police. I thought of being a bobby[3] myself when I left the Service, and I'd have done it but for the old lady. Now it's too late."

"The police are very good to us," said the Captain. "They took against us at first; but now there's nothing they won't do for the Army. They keep order at our holiness meetings and walk with us through rough streets. Yours is a rough place. We've often been pelted with rotten eggs and had water thrown on us in Wright Street."

"Rough's no name for it," groaned the caretaker. "You should come in some Saturday night; then it's like a madhouse. It was better once, for the gates were left open and the police walked through it, but the Company would have had to pay if it had been put on a bobby's beat,[4] so they ordered the gates to be shut at twelve o'clock. I'm there by myself, and if it hadn't been for my pal, I'd have had my head cut open long before this. I wish one of those committee gentlemen would spend a night on the Buildings. But they pocket the rents, and until there's a murder they'll make no difference."

"And they call themselves philanthropists!"

"I don't know what they call themselves; that's what they do, at any rate. And the ladies who collect the rents, they're a mistake. I don't mean to say they do the work badly, but women aren't made for rent-collecting, I take it. It would make your blood curdle to hear the names the tenants call them on Saturday nights. When a man's drunk he don't care a bit who he talks about, and the women are worse than the men in the names they call those poor ladies. I suppose the Company had them because they are cheap. It would come heavier to do the thing properly – I mean as Peabody's[5] do it, with

3   Slang word for the police. Sir Robert Peel (1788-1850), acting as Home Secretary under the Duke of Wellington's (1769-1852) Tory government of 1828-1830, founded the police force in London in 1829 with the passing of the Metropolitan Police Act. Thus, slang reference to the force refers back to the founder through the terms 'bobbies' and 'peelers'.

4   Under the 1868 Artisan's Dwellings Act, introduced to Parliament by independent Liberal William Torrens McCullagh (1813-1894), landlords could be forced by the local authority to repair or demolish slum property; the 1875 Artisans and Labourers Dwellings Improvement Act, introduced by Benjamin Disraeli's (1804-1881) Home Secretary for the Conservative parliament of 1874-1880, Richard Assheton Cross (1823-1914), enabled municipal authorities to compulsorily purchase slum dwellings and sell the land to developers to build better workers' housing. Because the new dwellings were built on private land they would not come under the beats of the Metropolitan Police and to have the buildings included would incur costs charged by the police force. As the East End Dwelling Company was part of the Four/Five Percent Philanthropy movement expenditure would be kept to a minimum to ensure the investors' return on their money and so George is left to deal with the disturbances alone.

5   The American banker and philanthropist George Peabody (1795-1869) founded

a caretaker and two men under him. The Company wouldn't like to spare money for that."

"I should think you'd be glad to leave it," said the Captain.

"Yes, I mean to better myself; but what's the good of leaving now?" asked George taking up the bit of parchment.

"You mustn't be hard on the lass," answered the little Captain. "I suppose when you were in the Service you had sweethearts. You've had more than one, I expect."

"That's different," replied the caretaker.

"Well, I don't see myself why women should have only one sweetheart and men half-a-dozen," remarked the Captain. "In the Army we have the same set of rules for both men and women. The General favours neither sex."

"In our service," said George, "it's different."

The little Captain looked at his watch; then he jumped off the table, saying that he must put on his uniform, that he had to conduct a meeting in a few minutes and must be there early, as his lieutenant had received a black eye the previous night, when a lot of roughs had come into barracks. The roughs had tried to upset the meeting, so he had been obliged to turn the ring-leader out, with the help of his lieutenant.

"We charged him," said the Captain, "and he's got a month. We were forced to make an example. The General doesn't like us to show fight if we can help it, but if roughs come in bent on mischief we must turn the ring-leader out."

"I wish I was your height," he continued, as the caretaker stood up; "it would be better for me – they'd show me more respect."

"You wouldn't have been taken into the real Service," said George. "But, I suppose, in your Army size doesn't matter, especially as you take in women."

The little Captain laughed, and when the caretaker had put his bit of parchment into his pocket, said, "Pray, I mean think over it. You need not decide all at once. Good night, and God bless you."

The caretaker thought it over for a couple of months. After that he went to see Nelly. He found her sitting in the sergeant's little kitchen, where the warm June sunshine came through the window, and some roses stood in a

---

the Peabody Trust to build dwellings for the respectable London poor, replacing some of the London slums. The first block of dwellings – rooms with shared kitchen and hygiene facilities – was opened in Spitalfields in 1864 and others followed in areas such as Islington, Bermondsey and Shadwell. George would presumably be familiar with the Whitechapel blocks running between what is now Royal Mint Street and East Smithfield along John Fisher Street, the street running parallel to Cartwright Street where Katherine/Charlotte's Buildings were located.

glass on a table. She looked very pale, very delicate. Her long red-brown hair fell over the back of the seat and covered her shoulders. She had on a simple black dress, an old one of the sergeant's.

When she saw George her face flushed scarlet, then she turned deadly pale and rested her thin cheek on her hand, while he took a seat on the opposite side of the fireplace. He sat twirling his hat, without speaking. On the way to the sergeant's house he had framed a speech; in fact, during the last two months he had thought of many things he would say to Nelly; but now that he found her looking so pale, so delicate, words forsook him. He was paying her rent, she was dependent upon him, she looked as if a breath of wind would blow her over. How could he say anything?"

At last he blurted out, "WHO IS IT?"

She hid her face in her hands.

"Who is it?" repeated the caretaker. "Jack thinks maybe it's that chap we met in Battersea Park. It if is," said George, getting up, "I'll smash every bone in his body; I'll thrash his very soul out."

He waited for Nelly to speak, and as he stood there asking "Who is it?" they heard a faint noise upstairs, the cry of a baby.

"Who is it?" demanded George, as Nelly sprang out of the chair. "Is it that man?"

"No," said Nelly, "it isn't."

She pushed past him and hurried towards the staircase, but she could not go up. She fell on the steps, and when George raised her in his arms he found that Nelly had fainted.

That evening she received another visit. Tom knocked at the door and asked to see his sister. He meant to be very magnanimous.

"Fust of all," he said to himself, "I'll tell 'er what I think of 'er, then I'll offer to take 'er back. She's fit for work now, and it's difficult to get on without 'er. We owe three weeks' rent. If she don't come 'ome, they'll send the brokers in upon us."

He walked into the kitchen, and there he found Nelly nursing her baby. The sergeant's wife[6] had gone out after she had opened the door for him, thinking, perhaps, that the brother and sister would like to be alone together. Nelly wished him a quiet "Good evening," and, as she spoke, the loafer felt that somehow or other a change had come over his sister, that she was no

---

6 Presumably an error. Nelly has been lodging with a female Salvation Army sergeant. The woman is a widow – described in the novel as 'the mother of six buried babies' – but there has been no mention of that sergeant's husband nor of any rank he may have held within the Army. This error was not corrected in the Author's Co-operative edition.

longer the Masher of the Buildings.

"Put down that brat while I talk to yer," said Tom; "I've summat to say, Nelly."

Instead of putting down the baby Nelly only held it closer. She rocked it in her arms while she waited for Tom to go on speaking, and held its tiny head to her face, kissing it.

"There's no denying," said Tom, "we've cause to complain. After all the airs yer gived yerself we'd a right to expect yer'd do different. Miss Marsh was quite taken back when she came for the rent, and mother told her about it. And Father O'Hara — "

"What did he say?" interrupted Nelly.

"Well, I forget; but I know he said summat."

There was a pause. Then the loafer continued, "Notwithstanding yer've behaved so badly, mother and I've made up our minds to let bygones be bygones. Yer can come back to the Buildings when yer've got rid of the baby."

"Got rid of the baby!" ejaculated Nelly.

"Well, we can't have that squalling brat in the shop. Yer can't expect it. You must put it out to nurse,[7] and when yer've done that we'll take yer back."

"Do you think I'd part with my baby?" cried Nelly, "my own little baby."

She looked lovingly at the small red face on her knee, the little shrunken fingers and the wrinkled neck about which she had already placed her coral necklace. She had dream of clothes her machine would make by-and-bye; of wonderful little cloaks and dresses her fingers would stitch. And as the looked she repeated, "'Tain't likely I'd part with my baby, my own, own little baby."

"Well, if yer won't part with that brat we'll put up with it," said Tom.

But Nelly hesitated.

"Yer can come home to-night and bring it along with yer. If yer put yer bits of things together I'll fetch the bundle; that's more than most brothers 'ud do for yer, I can tell yer."

"No," said Nelly, shaking her head, "I'll never come back to the Buildings."

"Yer wun't?"

"No, Tom, never."

7　Tom is referring to the practice of baby farming where a child (often an illegitimate child) is given to a woman ostensibly to nurse but with the implicit understanding that the child would die through neglect or starvation. George Moore (1852-1933) addressed the business of baby farming in *Esther Waters* (1894) when Esther unwittingly puts her baby out to nurse with the murderous Mrs. Spires. Nelly is worldlier than Esther and her refusal to 'part with my own baby' suggest she understands Tom's intention of a permanent parting through death.

CHAPTER IX

A CHRISTENING

It was some time before Nelly could find work again. Captain Lobe went to see the sweater's wife, hoping that she would take her best hand back; but although she missed Nelly she would not own it, she scoffed at the idea of having such a hand on her premises. The sweater did not look up from his ironing while Captain Lobe stood in the workroom; he left his wife to deal with hands, children and servants. He disapproved of the thong she kept in her pocket, but if one of the children hid under his table he told the child to "go and take it."

Captain Lobe left the house, having failed in his mission, but determined to find work for Nelly. He knew of no sweater belonging to the Salvation Army, although it boasted of men and women plying many trades, following a great variety of professions. A converted chemist had the previous evening begged people to take "the pill of salvation"; a shoe black had compared sinners with dirty boots, and saints with leather after if had been anointed with Day and Martin's blacking;[1] but no sweater had ever come to the penitent's bench that he was aware of, or sweater's wife either. He suggested that Nelly should make a pair of trousers for himself. They would give her something to do, he said; and when they were finished he would go in them to sweaters' houses. He saw nothing ridiculous in this sort of advertisement (there is probably no body of people so wanting in humour as the Salvation Army); he only thought how he could put the doctrines he preached into practice. At length he found work for her with a sweater in Bishopsgate – a man without a wife, who looked upon hands as human beings. Captain Lobe took Nelly to his shop, and she returned home with a bundle of trousers under her arm, feeling once more independent.

Those were very happy days for Nelly. She sat in the sergeant's little kitchen making trousers, with the baby in a cradle beside her. If she was tired of work she had the baby to look at, and after work was finished she took it out for a walk. When the sergeant came home at night she always had some important piece of news about it to communicate; it had smiled while she

---

1 A popular brand of boot polish developed by Charles Day (1782/3-1836) and Benjamin Martin (d. 1834).

dressed it, its hair had grown the hundredth part of an inch; it had only cried three or four times and then not much; a woman in the street had stopped to look at it. Many an hour the two women spent talking over babies; for the sergeant had "buried" six children, and knew all about infant ailments, also when babies cut teeth, how soon they ought to be vaccinated, the time for short and long petticoats.[2]

Nelly generally accepted the sergeant's advice about the management of her baby, but on one point they were at variance. Nelly said that her boy must be a Catholic – a believer in the virtues of holy water, the intercession of the Virgin Mary and the saints. The sergeant wished him to be a soldier, enrolled as a member of the Salvation Army from the very beginning.

"You're a Catholic," she told Nelly, "but that's no reason why your baby should be brought up in darkness. I don't say anything against your religion, but I should like the boy to begin right, seeing he has been born in my house."

Nelly felt the force of this argument, but she had not the courage to break through fixed habits. Besides, she was afraid to let the baby be baptized as a Protestant. She had heard of purgatory, and knew that all who died must enter there for years or minutes. If her baby died – Nelly shuddered – if it died she could not go with it, so she ought to place it under the protection of the Virgin Mary – give it a guardian angel. But she shrank from taking it to the Catholic Church. She had not seen Father O'Hara since she left the Buildings, and she was afraid to meet him. She put off the christening, although she felt that it was wrong to do so; she contented herself with talking about it. She knew that in case of illness babies may be christened by any "staid" person; that the sergeant might baptize her boy if he had a fit, convulsions, or any sudden attack that seemed dangerous. But for that purpose she must keep some holy water in the house; it would not do to use water that was not consecrated. How could she get holy water without going to the priest's for it? She puzzled her brains to answer this question, and at last she decided that she would pay Susan a visit. The lame girl had Lourdes water, which was the best water of all for christening babies. It was wonderful

2   The 1853 Vaccination Act had made smallpox vaccination compulsory for children within three months of birth. It had been tradition for centuries that, from birth to the ages of around four or five or even later, boys would be dressed in petticoats (very long dresses below the feet) or frocks (shorter and which allowed the child to walk). The act of dressing a boy in trousers (or breeching) would be a celebrated right of passage in the child's life. This practice of dressing boys the same as girls up to a certain age continued into the early twentieth century. Although the time for her child's vaccination would be regulated by the state, the time for breeching would be set by local cultural traditions and the sergeant's experience would guide Nelly.

stuff; it kept cold in the hottest place, it remained always fresh; it could not only christen babies, but cure them of illnesses too if the Blessed Lady wished it to do so. She would ask Susan for a little Lourdes water, she thought, then, if anything happened, the sergeant could christen the baby; if the worst came to the worst she would baptize it herself.

The evening of the day on which she made up her mind to visit Susan she set off for the Buildings with a bottle in her pocket. She waited about until it grew dark, then she went to the lame girl's place, hoping to slip in without being noticed; but around the door she saw a crowd of women and children. When she entered the little room she found it full of people. Susan lay in her low chair-bedstead, and one look at her face told Nelly that she was dying. Beside her, on a box, with his head in his hands, sat the shoeblack. His great dark eyes were fixed mournfully on his companion; he knew that she was about to leave the world in which she had been so afflicted. The women elbowed their neighbours, for Susan was delirious. She spoke of ice mountains, noisy rivers, grottoes and pilgrims. She whispered an Ave Maria. She talked to unseen presences – guardian angels.

Steps were heard in the passage. Father O'Hara stood at the door. He said a few words in Latin before he entered the room, then he walked in, followed by an acolyte. With a glance he cleared the place of everyone but the shoeblack and Nelly. They crept into a corner, whence they could see the priest anointing Susan's head, hands and feet. He repeated a Latin service and the acolyte said the responses, while Susan babbled of mountains and glaciers, rivers and grottoes, wholly unconscious of what was going on around her. Every minute her voice grew weaker, her arms refused to stretch themselves so far out, her head became more feeble, more stiff, but her face was radiant, a smile transfigured the features of the poor afflicted Catholic. Father O'Hara looked at her and crossed himself. Having done that he left the room, followed by the acolyte, without taking any notice of the sobbing shoeblack or speaking a word to Nelly. The women crowded about the dying girl directly he had gone down the staircase; they discussed the wake, talked of the funeral, and wondered who would have "the bits of things" Susan had to leave behind her.

Nelly returned home thinking about the ceremony she had witnessed, and asking herself if the holy oil with which the priest had anointed Susan would have had the same effect had she or Tim applied it. She came to the conclusion that Latin words said by a priest must be more efficacious than English words said by an ordinary man or woman; that it would be safest to let Father O'Hara baptize her baby. He always stood by the font at four o'clock on Sunday afternoons, ready to christen infants; she would gather up her courage and carry her baby to church the following Sunday, she said to herself. Purgatory was a very real place to Nelly. The Pope, she thought, had the key of it; priests were its jailers. The Virgin Mary could limit the time sinners must spend in torment by interceding with her Son for them; guardian angels hovered about good Catholics; but unbaptized babies – Nelly shivered when she thought of what happened to unbaptized babies.

The following day she was all the more determined to have her baby properly christened, because it did not seem quite the same as usual. She could not see or hear anything the matter with it but she FELT a change in its cries and movements. The sergeant noticed no difference. Nelly, however, who knew all her boy's ways and noises, was anxious about him. He slept, ate, and behaved as he had done from the day of his birth, yet she fully felt that it was a different baby.

"Perhaps," she said to the sergeant, "it's only because he's growing older."

She bought some cherry-coloured ribbons to tie his sleeves with, washed and ironed a long white robe the sergeant produced out of an old box in which were still kept some of the buried children's garments, and cut up a shawl of her own to make him a cloak. When all this finery was ready she dressed him and walked off with him to the Catholic church. Her love of smart things for herself had vanished; she never seemed to care now what she had on, to give her hats and feathers any attention; but she spent a great deal of time adorning her child.

The sergeant shook her head when she saw fresh ribbons and smart woollen shoes on the baby. She told Nelly it was a good thing that the child happened to be a boy.

Nelly promised not to buy any more infant toggery; but the next time she went out she was sure to see something unusually pretty – something she MUST purchase. She could do a few extra pairs of trousers to pay for an addition to the baby's wardrobe she said to the sergeant; and, curious to say, those extra pairs never made her tired or gave her a headache.

When she drew near the church that Sunday afternoon she became strangely agitated. The sense of peace and happiness she had experienced during the last few weeks changed to uneasiness. She stumbled on the doorstep, and on entering the church her mind became flooded with memories. She saw the place where she had made her first confession – the spot on which she had knelt when she had first received the Sacrament. These events had really happened, yet they seemed so far away they might have been the acts of another Nelly. Trembling and pale she dipped her fingers in holy water and made the sign of the cross on her baby's forehead. Then she went to the font and sat down to wait for Father O'Hara.

Sitting there she remembered that she had no sponsors for the baby; that she had entirely forgotten to find him godfather and godmother. The sergeant had refused to enter a Catholic church. Captain Lobe, had he been allowed by Army regulations to stand sponsor, would not have had time to do it. She had not thought of other godparents. She looked at the clock, and found that she had still ten minutes. But if she went out of church, who[3] should she fetch? Susan was dead; she had no friend now on the Buildings. She sighed when she thought of Jack, the costermonger's wife, and half-a-dozen more people who would have stood sponsors had things been different.

While she sat thinking, wondering if Father O'Hara would baptize her boy without godparents, she caught sight of the little shoeblack. He was burning candles for Susan, watching the flickering lights, and meditating on what he could do to lessen his sweetheart's time in purgatory. His face was very lugubrious. On the sleeve of his jacket he wore a bit of rusty crape, which he had bought in a rag-shop, another bid adorned his hat, a third was tied round his neck.[4]

"Tim," said Nelly, going up to him, "will you stand godfather to my child?"

The little shoeblack looked delighted. He greatly admired Nelly, and he thought it an honour to stand godfather to her baby. By his advice she asked the old woman who sold candles to be the baby's godmother, and after she[5] had negotiated the business, she took her place at the font among half-a-dozen other mothers and babies.

She bent down to unfasten her baby's bonnet and cloak, and when she looked up she saw Father O'Hara. He had come to the font unnoticed, and stood with his eyes fixed on her face. He seemed to be reading her thoughts, probing her conscience. She had confessed to him ever since she went to school; he knew her as well as any priest can know a human being – any man can know a woman. Lately she had kept away from him – he understood why – and he thought that he read in her face much less humility and self-abasement than he would have inculcated had she come to the confessional box. There was a pride of maternity on Nelly's countenance, a look of delight in her hazel eyes when she turned them on her boy, which the priest thought

---

3   Author's Co-operative Edition: whom.
4   Crepe was used in mourning dress and the removal of crepe was the signal for the move out of deep mourning. The shoeblack is in the earliest and deepest stage of mourning and is following mourning dress etiquette as far as his poverty will allow.
5   Author's Co-operative Edition: Nelly.

very sinful, very unholy. With a word to the acolyte, he separated Nelly from the other mothers, placed her on his left and wedding rings on his right.[6] At first Nelly did not recognize the difference, but when she saw the women gather in their petticoats and look coldly at her baby she realized what had happened – she had brought her boy into the world without consulting a priest about it, without letting him place on her finger the magic badge which makes it right to have babies.

"Name this child," said Father O'Hara, taking in his arms, last of all, Nelly's child.

"Arthur," replied the godparents.

The priest looked at Nelly; then the boy was baptized in the name of the Father, the Son, and the Holy Ghost, under the name of Arthur.

The service was soon finished, and nothing remained to be done but write in a book the names of the newly-baptized infants. Father O'Hara went to a little table and entered the children in a register without looking up, until he came Nelly's baby. Then he paused, fixed his solemn eyes on Nelly, and asked: —

"Whose child is it?"

"Mine," answered Nelly.

"The father's name?"

Nelly began to cry, but said nothing.

"The father's name is Arthur what?" asked the priest, throwing while he spoke a stern look at Nelly, and dipping his pen in the ink.

"He hasn't got a father; he's only got me," sobbed Nelly.

---

6   Nelly is not simply being separated from the married mothers but her position echoes that of the division between the blessed sheep and the unblessed goats in Matthew 25.31-33: 'When the Son of Man comes in his glory, and all the angels with him, he will sit on his glorious throne. All the nations will be gathered before him, and he will separate the people one from another as a shepherd separates the sheep from the goats. He will put the sheep on his right and the goats on his left.' The priest's positioning of Nelly exposes her unmarried state and separates her from the blessings given to the married mothers by both the priest and the Church.

CHAPTER X

THE BABY FALLS ILL

The next day there was certainly something the matter with the baby. The sergeant owned it, but could not say what it was. She advised Nelly to take the child to a chemist, who gave advice gratis, in return for which he expected patients to purchase pills or powders made on the premises. Nelly carried the baby to him and waited a long time in a small place at the end of his shop, where the sun beat through a closed window, and a hundred flies buzzed about, lean-looking creatures that fed on pills and powders and lived among surgical instruments. At last the chemist came in. He looked at the baby, and asked Nelly a few questions concerning it. He pulled it about, tapped its chest, examined its tongue, felt its pulse, then declared that there was nothing the matter with it, that Nelly was nervous.

"You keep it too clean," he told her. "Let it grub a bit."

Nelly had often heard mothers say in the Buildings that it was a mistake to keep children too clean, that babies did not thrive if kept too tidy. She knew that Whitechapel mothers contrasted their children with those they had nursed in service, and pitied the latter while they caressed their own dirty infants. It was all right to bathe children once a week, to wash their hands and face night and morning; to do more than that was very bad for their health, made them delicate, said East End ladies. Nelly had, however, a prejudice in favour of soap and water, inherited from her father most likely, for neither Tom nor her mother cared about such frivolities;[1] in fact, Tom had often called her love of cleanliness "ridiculus."[2] She shrank from the idea of letting her baby "grub a bit," much as a West End mother shrinks when a certain well-known medical baronet[3] suggests that bones should lie about the nursery for the children to suck. She left the shop with a packet of powders in her pocket, feeling anxious and nervous.

---

1 This could refer to either the dead man who was married to Nelly's mother or Nelly's illegitimacy. The note that Nelly's cleanliness comes 'most likely' from her father suggests that her father's attitude to hygiene is unknown and therefore reinforces the suggestion of her illegitimacy.
2 Author's Co-operative Edition: rediculus.
3 I have been unable to identify this reference but it is possible that Harkness had a specific medic in mind from her nursing days.

The baby grew daily worse. It lost flesh, its little limbs shrank, its face grew shrivelled, it became peevish and sleepless. Its constant cries hurt Nelly; yet she was forced to make trousers from morning to night. Often she was obliged to leave it whining in its cradle, instead of taking it on her knee, for the work must be done to buy its food and provide its medicine. At night she sat up with it; and at first she looked forward to the hours of darkness, knowing that she could then attend to all its wants; but soon the sleepless nights made her drowsy – nights and days grew both alike.

She had written to George directly after the Salvation Captain had found her work; and in the letter she had thanked him very humbly for his help; had told him rather proudly that she need not trouble him any more, as she was now able to support the baby and provide for herself. She had received no answer, and had heard nothing of the caretaker since she posted his letter; she did not like to write again, to tell him all she was suffering.

Perhaps if Captain Lobe had called to see her, something might have been done for the child but his time in Whitechapel had almost run its course and he was busy winding up accounts before he went to fresh barracks. So she must work; for the sergeant was poor like herself, and the sweater could not afford to keep a hand doing nothing, although he treated hands as human beings.

She worked slowly and pricked her fingers, because the baby often lay in her lap. Great tears splashed down on its forehead, its mother's hazel eyes were so weary. "If only I could bear the pain for you!" sobbed Nelly; "if only I could do ANYTHING for you, my poor little, wee boy!" She said Pater Nosters and Ave Marias while she fed the machine; she whispered prayers which would surely have touched the heart of the Virgin Mary had our Blessed Lady been able to hear them. She learnt the saddest of all sad lessons as she looked at her child – namely, that vicarious suffering is a boon denied to men and women, because our nature is such that we could make joy out of anguish, if only we might bear the pains and the sorrows of those we love. There is a theory current that East End mothers do not love as West End mothers love. Let those who believe it go down to Whitechapel, and there they will find love intensified, because love is dumb.

Acting upon the sergeant's advice, she carried her baby to a children's hospital in Whitechapel.[4] She went with it into a room full of mothers and

---

4   *Children's Hospital in Whitechapel*: Probably not the famous Hospital for Sick Children at Great Ormond Street, founded by Dr. Charles West (1816-1898) in 1851 and which enjoyed the patronage of influential figures such as Lord Shaftesbury, Angela Burdett Coutts and Edwin Chadwick, as this was situated in Bloomsbury. The hospital Nelly and her baby attend is presumably the hospital now known

children, and waited until her turn came to consult a doctor who sat at a table. The doctor listened to all she had to say about it, then he examined it carefully. The examination lasted several minutes; afterwards he told her to bring it again.

The next time she brought it he showed it to another man. Nelly listened eagerly to all they said about it, watched their grave faces, and tried to find out if they thought it very ill. But she could not discover much from their words or looks; and when the consultation was finished they merely told her to have some medicine made up for it, to let them see it the following week. The third time she took it the doctor said that he would like it left in the hospital.

"Alone?" exclaimed Nelly.

"You can come to see it twice a week," said the doctor, "and if it grows worse you will be allowed to remain with it altogether."

"Is it so very ill?" asked Nelly.

"We can tell you more about it when we have it in the hospital," answered the doctor.

"I can't leave it to-day," said Nelly, turning away from him. "I'll bring it to-morrow if it isn't better. I can't leave it this evening."

When the sergeant returned home from work she found the baby worse, and Nelly sitting with it in her arms, sobbing. Its tiny face had become drawn about the mouth, its feeble cries had grown shrill, it had refused to take its food, its head had fallen away when Nelly had tried to feed it. All that night the two women sat up with it; they talked in whispers when it dozed, and walked with it in turn up and down the kitchen.

The sergeant said the Nelly ought to have left it in the hospital, and tried to soothe her fears about strange nurses. "Even if you had no work to do, and could mind it properly, you ought to let it go where it can have the best food and doctors," she told Nelly. The mother knew that the sergeant was right, but when she looked at her baby she could not help doubting whether strangers could do what she did for it – watch it and love it every minute. It fell asleep in the early morning while the sergeant was making a cup of tea, and slept so peacefully Nelly hoped it was better. She would not feel the parting so much if she were less anxious about it, she told the sergeant, if only it looked brighter, and stopped crying. But directly it woke up it began to wail louder than before; it turned away when she tried to feed it; its little

---

as The Royal London Hospital, founded in 1740 as The London Infirmary and then known as The London Hospital from 1748. The original building was located in Featherstone Street, Moorfields but moved to Whitechapel Road in 1757 where it remains today.

limbs grew clammy and cold. She owned to herself that it would have been best to leave it in the hospital, that she had acted selfishly in bringing it home.

"Kiss it," she said, in a broken voice to the sergeant, as the mother of six buried babies prepared for her day's work; "it will be gone before you come back again."

She had every intention of starting for the hospital directly the baby's "bits of things" had been put together; but it took a long time to make up the bundle, and it was afternoon before she left the house. Then she walked slowly, lengthening out the minutes, putting off the moment of parting. The child had become drowsy; its head lay heavily on her shoulder, and its eyelids were closed. The little arms fell limply downwards; its little hands seemed to have lost all their strength; its little fingers were stretched out instead of curling up as usual.

Nelly often stopped to look at it, and each time she looked, a terrible, sinking feeling came over her, a feeling called in Whitechapel "heart-ache." She sat down on the hospital doorstep before she went in, knowing that this was the last time she would have the baby all to herself for days, perhaps for weeks, wanting to say good-bye to it before she left it among strangers, wishing to give it a good-bye kiss which none but our Blessed Lady and its guardian angel would witness. As she sat there a carriage stopped at the door, and a lady – "a great lady" Nelly called her – stepped out of it; a tall, stately woman, with a long, thin neck, high shoulder-bones, and skin like parchment. Nelly looked at the lady, and while she was looking a powdered footman said, "make way for her ladyship." Nelly rose up, and followed the lady through the hospital doors into a room full of babies, when a nurse, in blue dress, smart apron and cap, spotless collar and cuffs, hastened to welcome "her ladyship."

"Sis – ter, how co – ld you – r hands a – re," said the visitor, in a languid voice, as she shook hands with the nurse. She made the same remark every time she came to the hospital, in summer or winter, and the sister always answered "yes." She was a pretty woman, this sister; a little widow, who had taken to nursing because she was poor – because she thought a nurse held a better position in the eyes of the world than a governess.[5]

She knew that many rich ladies try to get rid of *ennui* in hospitals, but no rich ladies made the same experiment in schoolrooms. She had relations in the House of Commons, a cousin in the House of Lords, and connections in all the professions, more especially, she was wont to say, in the army. She

---

5 Harkness had initially trained as a nurse before leaving the profession to take up journalism and authorship (see Biography for further details). It was her decision to give up nursing in favour of writing that caused the final rift between herself and her family and her father's withdrawal of financial support.

was always afraid that people were forgetting her rank – was on thorns about her social position; and she had reasons for this most likely, considering the odd drops the social scales give when people have large pretensions and little money. Thus she welcomed "a great lady" into her ward, and gracefully acknowledged that her hands were always cold, that from childhood she had suffered from cold fingers. She spoke to "the great lady" with a lisp, almost a drawl; in quite a different voice from the one she used when talking to patients or nurses, even to doctors.[6]

This hospital for women and children was quite an aristocratic place, although in Whitechapel. It had a Prince as its president, noblemen on its committee, and endless titled ladies for visitors. Occasionally a Princess paid it a visit; then the young doctors danced attendance, the committee spread out a red carpet, the matron bowed and scraped, and the secretary wrote a long report of the Royal visit to a newspaper, in which he said that the Princess seemed quite at home in the place, was evidently great friends with the matron, and had been induced to visit the hospital by young Dr. —— , the son of the well known Dr. —— , of —— Street.

"The great lady" turned away from the sister, and walked down the ward to the bed of a little boy – "a sweet little sufferer" she called him. She took a chair, and drew out of her pocket a camphor lozenge, a bottle of salts, and a scented pocket-handkerchief. This gave the sister time to notice Nelly, who stood at the door silently watching what was going on around her. The room seemed to her very like a large doll's house, such as she had seen in West End shop windows, only it was larger, the nurses moved about, and the children made a noise. Everything in the room was perfect. The walls were ornamented with all sorts of devices, the doors had painted panels, the tables were covered with flowers, the floor was stained to match the doors and windows. Nurses tripped in and out, wearing dainty dresses, roses at their throats, and steel instruments at their waists. Children played with costly toys sent from Royal nurseries, and looked at picture-books made up by West End ladies. Everything was pretty to look at except the little suffering faces in some of the cots, pleasant to hear but the cries of pain which came from a few cradles.

Just as the sister advanced towards Nelly a noise was heard, and "the great lady" rose in haste from her chair. She had found the "sweet little sufferer" asleep, and had fancied that he had fainted, thereupon she had put her scent

---

6   (Harkness's footnote) 'I trust my readers will not fail to recognize this sister as an exceptional member of the noble band of hospital nurses; for which no one has a greater respect than myself.'

bottle under his nose, and he, roused out of his dreams, had struck out at "her ladyship." In the confusion that followed Nelly was forgotten. It was only after "the great lady" had said, "How co – ld you – r hands a – re, sister," and had gone to her carriage, that the sister had time to inquire what Nelly wanted.

"Please, ma'am," said Nelly, "have you had a baby?"

The sister stared at the speaker. She looked at Nelly's hand, glanced at the rim of gold on her own finger, and asked, haughtily, "Is the child a patient?"

"Is there NO ONE here who has had a baby?" inquired Nelly, in a trembling voice. "The doctor said I must leave my child in the hospital, but I thought I'd be sure to find a nurse that had had a baby."

The sister did not condescend to make any reply. She thought Nelly mad or tipsy, for otherwise, she said to herself, an East End woman would scarcely dare to ask such an impertinent question of a West End lady. She told a nurse to take the baby and send the mother away. Then she went into her room and shut the door.

"Have you had a baby?" Nelly asked a girl in uniform.

The nurse blushed, and answered, "No."

"Have NONE of you had babies?" she repeated, after she had watched the nurse lay the baby in a cradle, "NONE of you?"

The nurse looked annoyed, and said that she should call the sister if Nelly stayed any longer, that the mother must kiss her baby and go.

"Oh, don't call that sister," sobbed Nelly, kissing the little white face on the pillow. "She couldn't look and speak like that if she had had a child of her own. How can women understand babies that have never had 'em? I wish I'd kept him at home."

CHAPTER XI

A CHILDREN'S HOSPITAL

She went slowly out of the ward downstairs into the hall. There she stopped to speak to the porter. She asked him when she would be allowed to visit her baby; and he, seeing tears in her eyes, said that she might come early next morning. He had children at home, so he knew a little of what she was feeling. He tried to cheer her, and told her that the doctors would have allowed her to remain if they had thought her child's illness dangerous. "It's a good sign that you mayn't stop," he said. "I had a child in here once, and they made my missus bide the first night along with it, though, like you, she didn't suckle her infant.[1] You see, they thought my kid might die sudden; but they don't think so with your boy. Cheer up, young woman; you'll find him better in the morning."

Nelly left the hospital, looking back as she went, feeling her arms very empty now she had no baby in them. The streets were full of noisy men and women, so she wandered towards the river. She could not make up her mind to go home to face the lonely kitchen, to look at the empty cradle. She sat down on a large triangle of grass, around which she saw boats, barges, and vessels with and without masts.[2]

The craft reminded her of the days she had spent on the river with Mr. Grant. The memory of those days brought with it no bitterness, it was not in Nelly's nature to feel bitter against anybody. She did not blame herself much; she only wished she had acted differently. As to Mr. Grant she scarcely gave him a thought, he seemed to far off. "Besides," said Nelly, "it wasn't all his fault."

Presently it began to rain, and she went into a shed until the storm

---

1 Nelly does not breastfeed her baby. A suckling child could not be separated from its mother while she was breastfeeding and so it would be necessary for the mother to stay in the hospital with the child. Nelly and the porter's wife would not be allowed to stay unless the child was in danger as any nurse could bottle-feed a child.

2 Oliver's Island at Kew is the Thames island that fits this description the best. The island was used in the nineteenth and early twentieth centuries for building and repairing barges, hence the 'vessels with and without masts'. However, this is a long way from The (Royal) London Hospital – or any of the London hospitals – so Nelly would be unable to see either the building or its light from the island.

was over. She could see the hospital from the place where she sat, and she wondered which window stood above the baby's cot. The window, must, she thought, be rather high up, because she had mounted so many steps to reach the ward. "It is one of the top windows," she said to herself, "somewhere near the roof." While she was looking at the hospital a light appeared in a tower above it. Nelly clasped her hands together and gave a sigh of relief. Now I'll know just where my baby is," she murmured; "I'll not quite lose sight of it."

She took her beads out of her pocket and began to say an Ave Maria. Soon they dropped on her lap. She fell asleep, and slept a disturbed sleep, broken by starts, but out of which she could not rouse herself. For several weeks she had not had a good night's rest; now she was thoroughly exhausted. The baby no longer needed her constant attention; she could do nothing but wait. In her dreams she seemed to see it smiling as it used to smile before its face changed so much, stretching out its little hands and feet, crowing, and making the strange music which mothers alone find melodious. She thought that she heard it crying when she woke up, and she put out her hand to rock its cradle. She drew her hand quickly back, for there was no cradle there, only something hard and cold – a plank.

"Where am I?" she exclaimed, starting up. "What is it?"

She could see a lamp in the distance, and she groped her way towards it. She started when she reached the lamp-post, for all around her was water, nothing but water. The light shone feebly on the triangle of grass, and washing against its walls was the river, grim and dark. A few weird-looking masts were visible, coloured lights were dotted about, otherwise all was darkness. She was on an island, and there was no way of getting off; she must stay on it until the morning.

Nelly was not timid, but the idea of spending a night thus made her tremble. She had gone to sleep in the shed; no one had noticed her; the drawbridge had been lifted. Was she alone? If she was she did not mind; but supposing she was not? She shook all over as women shake then they realize their feebleness and masculine strength. She was not afraid of ghosts, only of her own weak muscles opposed to brute force and loneliness. She would have expressed her feelings somewhat differently, but this was what she dreaded as she looked at the shed out of which she had just crept, and then at the lights and the masts on the river. All at once she raised her eyes up, and there, opposite, she saw the lamp above the hospital. Her fears vanished. She sat down close to the wall, and, fixing her eyes on the light, she said an Ave Maria.

So the night passed. She could not sleep any more, but she listened to the city clocks as they chimed the hours, and she counted the minutes until she would see her baby. Was he asleep? Were the nurses good to him? If only she could have found anyone in that place who had been a mother, who had had a baby! What could single women know about children? How could married women understand babies if they had never had them?

"It's cruel and wicked," said Nelly, "it's cruel and wicked to let women nurse children that have never had them."

Morning rose cold and grey above the river, showing the barges and boats anchored near the triangle of grass upon which she sat. The lamp went out in the tower of the hospital, and the coloured lights disappeared one by one until the last was extinguished. A mist hung about the river, and when the sun made its appearance the grass was covered with dew-drops. Nelly got up, feeling very cold and stiff. She ought to have been hungry, for she had had nothing to eat since the previous morning, and then she had only eaten some cold potatoes. But she had no appetite, her head ached, she felt faint; if she had had breakfast set out before her she could not have eaten it. When the drawbridge was lowered she ran across, heedless of questions, and made her way to the hospital, where she found the door open. She went quickly up the staircase to the ward and stood still on the threshold. The sister was busy fastening some steel instruments to her waist, the nurses were flitting about, washing and dressing children, preparing breakfast. No one noticed Nelly, and she went straight to her boy's cradle.

It was empty!

She started back, turned pale as the little white sheet she had lifted, and stared round the room. Then she tottered up to the sister, and asked, "What have you done with my baby?"

The sister dropped her steel instruments to look at the East End mother, and Nelly's eyes made her hesitate. "He has been very ill in the night," she said, "very much worse."

"Where is he?" demanded Nelly.

The sister answered, "I will show you."

She led the way downstairs, through the hall, into the basement. There she paused, with her hand on a door, and said, slowly, "you must be prepared for the worst. You child has been very ill in the night, very ill indeed."

"Open the door, you cruel woman," cried Nelly. "Let me go to my boy."

"He is dead," the sister said, slowly.

"Dead! dead!" cried Nelly. "You lie!"

The sister opened the door of a small, dark room. It was beautifully decorated. If death could be rendered loveable, that little mortuary would have made mourners love life's great enemy, instead of hating it. "There is a Reaper whose name is Death"[3] was written in front of the entrance, and upon the walls flowers and grass, corn and poppies, scarlet berries covered with hoar frost, were painted.

A small altar stood in the east, and on it were two tall, lighted candles and the Book[4] which gives hope that mothers will again meet their little ones, that fathers will one day see their lost children. The room had only one occupant, held but one dead baby.

Nelly paused for a minute, then went to a little coffin on tressels and bent down to look into it. As she looked an expression of awe and astonishment came over her face. The child was like wax – so exquisitely delicate, so marble-like. Again and again she looked. She put her ear to its mouth.

"It isn't dead," she said. "It can't be dead. It's only sleeping."

She took it out of the coffin and sat down with it on the altar steps. There she felt it carefully all over, undid its flannel shroud, examined its pale lips, its long dark eyelashes. She held it up to her cheek. She did not believe it was dead until she kissed it.

Then she opened her mouth and showed the astonished sister what it is to be an East End mother. She made the West End lady shiver and shake, for she vowed that the nurses had killed her boy, and she swore the most terrible oaths against childless wives and unmarried women who dared to call themselves nurses. Her bonnet dropped on the ground, her red-brown hair fell over her shoulders, her hazel eyes glittered as she shook her fist at the sister.

"Take that!" she said, and with one blow she knocked the childless nurse to the ground.

Then she wrapped her shawl round the little stiff, cold body, and ran with it out of the mortuary, up the staircase. The sister lay on the floor. The porter was having his breakfast. No one stopped her, until she reached the street. There a voice asked her: —

"What's the matter?"

---

3   The first line of the Henry Wadsworth Longfellow (1807-1882) poem 'The Reaper and the Flowers,' published in the *Knickerbocker*, January 1839 and subtitled 'A Psalm of Death'. The poem presents the reaping of grain and flowers as a metaphor for the death of age (the bearded grain) and youth (flowers) and gives comfort to those who are mourning the loss of children as the Reaper takes the cut flowers to Paradise. Stanza 6 gives hope to the grieving mother: 'And the mother gave, in tears and pain,/The flowers she most did love;/She knew she should find them all again/In the fields of light above.'
4   The Bible.

She looked up and saw Mr. Grant. He was coming into the hospital for a few hours' work, with a black bag (a thing he detested) in his hand, and his head full of psychological studies. At first he did not recognize Nelly. He had not seen her for months; and she had slipped from his memory. The novel he was writing exhausted so much of his energies he found his domestic life all-sufficient; he had not time to think about "hands" in Whitechapel. Directly Nelly lifted her head up, he knew her; and he was struck by her changed looks, her haggard face and tired eyes.

"What is it, Nelly?" he asked, with a touch of the old tenderness.

"It's your baby," said Nelly.

She fell down at his feet, exhausted; and when she opened her shawl he saw the little child dead in its shroud.

CHAPTER XII

"WHAT CAN I DO FOR HER?"

Of course he was dreadfully sorry. He tried to walk it off, to row it off, to drown it in champagne and whisky. That night tears came into his eyes when he looked at his West End baby. He was very proud of his tears – they were sentimental as those of a German lover.[1] His wife thought that he had a touch of fever, and laid her cool[2] hands on his forehead. For a moment he felt inclined to tell her about the "hand" in Whitechapel. He thought of Rousseau's confession to Thérèse after the adventure in the Rue des Moineaux.[3] He often compared his wife to Thérèse and himself to Rousseau. But he remembered that Thérèse was not an Englishwoman with strong maternal instincts; that his wife as a mother *par excellence*. That was shy she suited him so exactly, he said to himself. Artistic nature always wanted practical, phlegmatic complements. No; he would say nothing to his wife about the drive from the hospital to the sergeant's house. It made him shudder to think of it. Nelly had sat like a stone, and had shrunk away when he tried to comfort her. Her eyes had remained fixed on the little dead child opposite. Only once had she said anything, that was when the cab jolted. Then she had given a scream and had cried out to the cabman: —

"Oh, take care, you'll hurt it."

Poor little Nelly! her face had had such a hopeless expression when the reached the kitchen. She had not cried; but she had looked unutterably miserable as she placed the dead baby[4] in the empty cradle.

What could he do for her? He must do something.

---

1   A reference to Johann Wolfgang von Goethe (1749-1832), *The Sorrows of Young Werther* (1774), the story of Werther's doomed love for the beautiful peasant girl, Lotte.

2   Author's Co-operative Edition: cold.

3   Jean Jacques Rousseau (1712-1778) and Thérèse Levasseur (1721-1801) lived as common-law husband and wife for 33 years and had five children. Rousseau recounts in *The Confessions of Jean Jacques Rousseau* (1782) his drunken infidelity with the mistress of the minister Klupssel, who lived on the Rue de Moineaux, and the forgiveness of his actions by Thérèse. Arthur Grant identifies with Rousseau's infidelities but realizes his wife would not be as forgiving as Thérèse.

4   Author's Co-operative Edition: body.

The next day he called at the sergeant's house. He arrived rather late, for he had been obliged to put some hospital accounts straight, and to attend a committee meeting before he started. When he knocked, the door was opened by the little Salvation Captain, who looked gravely at him, and said that Nelly was busy. He could hear her machine in the kitchen. "Hands" must work, even if they have dead babies.

"Can't I see her, then?" he asked the Captain.

"I think you had better not," Captain Lobe answered. "Why should you? What good would it do?"

Mr. Grant looked at the little fellow in uniform, and repeated, "What good would it do?"

"No good," said the Captain, coming out of the house, and slamming the door.

"Which way are you going?"

"Back to barracks. My time's up to-morrow. This is my last evening in Whitechapel. To-night I give my farewell address. I say good-bye to my people."

The little Captain's face was very earnest, and Mr. Grant liked the look of it. He had a prejudice against the Salvation Army,[5] but Captain Lobe had such kind eyes, such a genial expression, he could not help wondering what sort of stuff such little Captains are made of. He began to talk of the Army, hoping to lead up to Nelly.

"May I walk with you?"

"Certainly," Captain Lobe answered.

"Where are you next quarters?"

"I don't know. I was with the General this morning and he asked me how I should like to go to America. I said I would rather stay in the old country, but I can't tell what he will do with me. I may get orders to leave England to-morrow, so I have been to see my mother's grave, and now I have only got to pack up."[6]

"How long have you been in the Salvation Army?"

"Two years. I joined it because I found less hypocrisy in it than in other religions, and I shall leave it directly I find anything better."

"Do you know Widgett, an Oxford man, who joined the Army and left it six months afterwards?"

---

5 The Salvation Army's work to alleviate the suffering of the poor would work against the principles of self-help propounded by both Liberals and Radicals and was perceived by some socialists as drawing the sting of poverty and therefore acting as a palliative against revolution.

6 Author's Co-operative Edition: I have only to pack up.

"Oh, yes; I knew him. He was too grand for the Army. He was always afraid of soiling his fingers. We go down among the people. Widgett wanted them to come up to us."

"Where did you get your training?"

"We have a college. This book will tell you all about it."

The little Captain took a thin red book out of his pocket and gave it to Mr. Grant, who opened it and read that officers were ordered to take a cold bath every morning, eat light suppers, and wear flannel.

"I see you go in for fire and brimstone,"[7] he said, turning to a much-thumbed page. "I never can understand how people reconcile these things with love and mercy. How do they manage it?"

"By the blood of Jesus," said the little Captain, lifting his cap.

Mr. Grant looked at him; then said, "I'm an agnostic."

"You might be worse."

They walked on in silence; for the Captain was thinking of his farewell address, and Mr. Grant was wondering how he could lead up to Nelly. The two men formed a great contrast. The hospital treasurer looked handsome and languid; his face showed that he had come to the end of everything, had experienced (so far as he was able) all sensations. Captain Lobe looked a mere boy beside Mr. Grant; his expression showed knowledge without experience, his voice had the thrill which touches hearts and unlocks secrets, his manner was that of an enthusiast.

"Have you known Nelly Ambrose long?" Mr. Grant asked at length.

"About two months."

"May I ask how you came across her?"

Captain Lobe then told him how the caretaker had brought Nelly to the Rescue Lassies' Room. He described things just as they had happened, without making any comment, and ended by saying that she was a good lass – a very good lass.

"I thought she was going to be married," said Mr. Grant.

"Her sweetheart was very much cut up about the baby," replied the Captain. "I hope, now it's dead, he will go to the poor lass; but I have not had time to let him know that she has lost it, and she is not likely to tell him

---

7   In Revelations 21.6 the saved and unsaved are separated for eternity after the millennium and the unsaved condemned to the burning lake in the second death: 'But the fearful, and unbelieving, and the abominable, and murderers, and whore-mongers, and sorcerers, and idolaters, and all liars, shall have their part in the lake which burneth with fire and brimstone: which is the second death.' The term 'fire and brimstone' is used in this instance in reference to the worship of a vengeful God and preaching the threat of everlasting damnation.

herself."

"Why not?"

"Do you think she has no feelings?"

Mr. Grant was silent. He had thought that "hands" took babies as a matter of course; he had imagined that babies made very little difference to East End sweethearts. When the Captain told him about George's visit and the bit of parchment, he was very much touched; all the more so because Captain Lobe made him no reproach. He began to realize the caretaker's feelings; to be afraid he had worked a life-long trouble for Nelly.

"I wish I could do anything for her," he said.

The little Captain remained silent.

"I think I had better call on the caretaker."

"No; don't do that. He's a very strong chap."

Mr. Grant laughed.

"If he had wanted to fight he would have found me out before this."

"He does not know that you are the baby's father. Nelly has always told him that you are not. She said this morning that she was afraid he would do you some mischief; that she had told a lie about it. She is a Roman Catholic."

Mr. Grant could not help smiling as the old Protestant prejudice crept to the surface; but the smile vanished when he realized that Nelly had kept his name secret – that she had tried to shield him from what she thought dangerous. Her pale face rose before him, so different from the face he had seen in the parks and on the river; an older, sadder face. He called himself by some bitter names when he thought of it – when he realized what a heavy price she had paid for a few hours' amusement.

"Can't I do anything for her?" he asked.

"You might pay for the funeral," the Captain suggested. "She is very poor, and she was saying this morning that she was afraid the baby would have to buried by the parish.[8] If you like you can send her a five-pound note."

"I will take it at once."

"No; you had better send it."

"Perhaps you are right," said Mr. Grant, slowly. "Here are the barracks."

"Won't you come in?" Captain Lobe asked.

---

8   To be too poor to afford a funeral and therefore to rely on a 'pauper's burial' paid for by the municipal authorities. The parish or local council were required, through public health needs, to bury the dead unable to pay for private funeral arrangements but costs were kept to a minimum and a pauper's funeral often meant that the body would be interred in an unmarked, mass grave. To a society so concerned with the customs and rites surrounding death this was the ultimate indignity and to be avoided at all costs (see Chapter I, Note 16).

Mr. Grant followed the little Captain into a hall full of people; and took a place under the gallery. The room was crowded. On a raised platform sat the officers; and below them stood a table surrounded by benches. Captain Lobe's face literally shone with benevolence as he made his way thought the men and women. He stopped to speak to a row of girls half-way up the room; then he jumped on the table. He gave out a hymn and led it himself, while the soldiers played on brass instruments. All the congregation helped to sing it; and Mr. Grant found himself joining in the chorus, which was set to popular music. Beside him sat a girl with rough hair and a dirty face, beating time on a pewter pot. In front were three men in flannel neckties and fustian,[9] who evidently thought the whole thing a joke, and made inquires about the state of one another's souls between the verses. The congregation was composed entirely of Whitechapel refuse; for the lowest of the low patronize the Army, people who refuse to enter chapels or churches go to Salvation Barracks.

After the hymn was finished, Captain Lobe requested a newly-converted member to speak; and a girl came to the table. She told the people how she had been saved; and the men and women nudged one another, for she was a well-known character in Whitechapel. Her manner was rather theatrical; it was easy to see that she was very excited, but she was evidently in earnest. She spoke of hell-fire, and the blood which save sinners from it, as though the things were realities; and more than one woman grew grave while she spoke; even the mockers looked serious.

Then the little Captain stood upon the table to say farewell to Whitechapel. First he spoke to the officers – his family he called them. He told them that he was a very young father, but that he had tried to do his duty – to act the part of a parent. "We shall not meet again on earth, perhaps," he said; "but, brothers and sisters, we shall meet in Heaven." Afterwards he turned to his "dear, dear people." "I had always heard that Whitechapel was a terrible place before I lived in London," he said, looking fondly down upon them. "I came here expecting a lot of trouble, but I was mistaken. If it were the will of God I would like to live always in Whitechapel."

"My hands are clean of your blood," he continued, solemnly. "I have told you the truth without flinching; I have warned you of hell and spoken of Heaven, as these things are written in the Bible. Come, come, my dear people, if there is one among you who is not saved – who is not at peace with Jesus – come to the table."

---

9   Fustian is a course cloth originally made of cotton and flax and later a dark, twilled cotton; flannel cloth is made from wool and might be coarse or fine, *OED*. The cloth used for the clothing of the three men signifies their poverty and working-class status.

"Almost persuaded to believe!" sand the officers, softly. "Almost persuaded Christ to receive."[10]

"Let us pray," said the little Captain.

Mr. Grant looked at his watch and found it was almost nine o'clock. He had forgotten his dinner. The little Captain's earnest face must have had a powerful influence to make him do that. He took up his hat, but before he could leave the room the Captain again began speaking.

"My time here is up to-night," he said. "To-morrow I go to other barracks. I wish that I could have left my accounts straight; yet I can't. I'm in debt. The gas bill is not paid yet, and I do not know how to pay it. I want three pounds, and it is not likely that the collection this evening will bring me in more than a few shillings. I have put half of my pay towards it, and the officers have made a special collection out of their own pockets. You, too, will be generous; I know you will be generous."

He spoke with a good deal of reluctance, and his face showed how glad he would be to have a clean billet. Mr. Grant put his hand in his pocket, and finding little there, walked towards the vestry.

"Have you got saved?" a pale-faced youth asked him, when he entered the room.

"No, not exactly," he answered. "But you can give my card to the Captain and say that I will pay the gas bill."

As he left the hall the Salvationists were singing a hymn. Six penitents knelt beside the table, and the officers waved their pocket-handkerchiefs over them, defying the devil. He had not gone far down the Whitechapel Road before he heard some one running after him, and, turning round, he saw Captain Lobe.

"God help you!" said the little fellow, seizing both of his hands; "God help you!"

"I will send you a cheque to-night," Mr. Grant told him, "and another for Nelly Ambrose."

The Captain lifted his cap, and with another "God help you!" went back to his people.

Mr. Grant walked on home – thinking.

---

10 The first two lines of the hymn 'Almost Persuaded' by Philip Paul Bliss (1838-1876) which opens '"Almost persuaded" now to believe;/"Almost persuaded" Christ to receive'. The hymn is a call for the 'almost persuaded' to fully embrace the teachings of Christ and is based on Marcus Vipsanius Agrippa's reply to Paul's defence against the accusation of the Jews in Acts 26.28 that 'Almost thou persuaded me to be a Christian.' To be almost persuaded is to be as far from salvation as any unbeliever.

CHAPTER XIII

A FUNERAL AND A WEDDING

A few days later a carriage drove up to the sergeant's house. Two men with white scarfs[1] round their hats brought it; and one of them went into the kitchen, when the door was opened, to fetch a little coffin. Nelly followed. She was alone, for the sergeant could not get a holiday, and Captain Lobe had gone to America. Her face was colourless, white as the wreath of roses she carried; its expression was so lonely, so despairing, passers-by stopped a minute to look at it; a crowd of boys and girls stared in at the window after she stepped into the carriage.

"No, don't put it there," said Nelly, when the man was about to place the little coffin under the box-seat. "Let me have it inside the carriage."

"It's the last time I'll mind it," she said, seeing the man hesitate. "To-morrow I'll have no baby."

The carriage went slowly along the Whitechapel Road towards the cemetery.[2] Many mourners had sat in it before Nelly; but not one had felt more hopeless and desolate. Cut off from the past, seeing no hope from the future, she did not seem to care what happened to her now she had lost the baby. Girlish pleasures seemed such silly things. She had no wish now for theatres and outings. She put her hand on the little coffin when the carriage jolted; and cold tears fell down her cheeks, quivered on her heavy eyelids.

At last the carriage left the dusty highroad and entered the cemetery. There a sense of peace came over the East End mother, for it lay like an oasis amid the dirty houses and tall chimneys; it was full of flowers and covered

---

1   White scarfs and white gloves worn by pallbearers, instead of the usual black crepe, indicated the burial of a child or young person.

2   The three cemeteries along the Whitechapel Road closest to Katherine/Charlotte's Buildings – Brady Street, Alderney Road and Mile End – are all Jewish cemeteries and so not the destination for Catholic Nelly's baby. The most likely burial place is the public Tower Hamlets Cemetery, which opened in 1841 or, a little further away, Victoria Park Cemetery, opened in 1845. A series of parliamentary Acts in the 1850s regulated the interment of bodies in London after public health concerns were raised about the small, crowded urban cemeteries. Both Tower Hamlets and Victoria Park Cemeteries were opened in less crowded areas outside of the close urban sprawl of London.

with grass. "After all, it's the best place for him," thought Nelly. "He might have been unhappy like me."

The little coffin was carried into a chapel and placed on tressels before the altar. Then, after a priest had read part of the funeral service, it was taken to a grave. "*Memento homo quia Pulvis es, et in pulverem reverteris*,"[3] said the priest; but there was something consoling in the way he said the words, something which carried Nelly's thoughts to the Heaven she believed in, which made her picture her child far away from noisy, suffering, hard-working Whitechapel. A soft wind moved the boughs of the trees, blew fallen rose-leaves into the grave. Nelly placed her wreath upon the little coffin. She did not cry when the earth fell on her baby. She went to the chapel, and there she knelt down to pray for him. Catholics are happier in one respect, at any rate, than Protestants; they can do something for their lost relations; the living and the dead in the Catholic faith are not divided.

When she reached home she found, to her great surprise, George, the caretaker, upon the doorstep. He helped her out of the carriage and asked if he might come into the house.

"I've got something to say," he told her, as they went downstairs into the kitchen, "something very particular."

Nelly's eyes filled with tears while she answered, in a choked voice, "yes." She had caught sight of the empty cradle. George sat down in a chair with his back to it, and said that he would like a cup of tea. He looked on while Nelly lighted the fire and filled the kettle, and his eyes softened as they had been wont to do when he met his sweetheart in the Buildings. Her face was older and had lost its freshness, but the hazel eyes were the same as ever, the red-brown hair seemed even more luxurious than before, the blue shadows still hovered about the white throat. Nelly's simple black dress gave a pathos to her movements which the caretaker could not resist. When the cup of tea was finished he said: —

"Come here, Nell."

She took her old place on his knee, but, instead of putting her arms round his neck, she crossed her hands on his shoulder, and when her cold cheek touched his forehead he felt her shivering.

"I think I'll have a pipe," he said. "Perhaps, Nell, you'll fill it."

She did as he suggested.

"I've bettered myself," he said, after he had puffed away for a few minutes.

---

3   From Genesis 3.19, 'Remember, man, you are dust and to dust you will return,' used in both funeral rites and the Catholic liturgy when ash is placed on the foreheads of the faithful.

"I'm going to leave the Buildings."

"Where are you going?" asked Nelly, closing her hands on the arm around her waist.

"Into the country. There's a society, or a club, just started, I don't know quite what they call it, but it's made up of people who write books. They've got a lot of little cottages, about an hour out of London;[4] and they want some one to look after the gardens, and — and — "

"And what?" inquired Nelly.

"Some one else to look after the servants.

"It's a very nice place," continued the caretaker; "and a lot cleaner than the Buildings.

"'We're casuals, too,' the gentleman said, when I went to look at it.

"'You're a cut above those in Whitechapel,' I told him.

"He laughed, and said I needn't be afraid but I'd get my wages, though authors were poor folks, and had difficulties in making both ends meet. The caretaker's house stands in the middle of the little cottages, and all the food's to be cooked in it. The meals are to be carried to the cottages by servants – two servants, Nelly. I'm to keep the gardens tidy, and take care of the keys when the places aren't let. All the cottages are took already; and they want me to go there at once. So I've told the committee that I've bettered myself, and next week I'm off."

Nelly remained silent.

"Fill another pipe," said George, wiping his forehead with a pocket-handkerchief. "It's wonderful how words come when one's mouth's got something in it; when mine's empty words seem to stick in my throat."

---

4   Probably based on Edward Carpenter's (1844-1929) home at Millthorpe, Der-
byshire. Set in a remote location between Sheffield and Chesterfield, Carpenter was
host to many authors, writers and advocates of new and advanced lifestyles including
sexologist Henry Havelock Ellis (1859-1939), socialists John (1859-1920) and Katherine (1867-1950) Bruce Glasier for part of their honeymoon, and Harkness's friend,
author and social theorist Olive Schreiner (1855-1920). For the first fifteen years at
Millthorpe, Carpenter was 'handicapped by the presence of a small working-family
in the house' (Carpenter, *My Days and Dreams* (London: George Allen & Unwin,
1916) p.150). These working families – first Albert Fearnehough (n.d.) and his family, then George Adams (d. 1910) and his – would work at Millthorpe, the men helping Carpenter with his market garden and sandal-making and the women carrying
out the domestic labour. It was not until Carpenter met George Merrill that his need
for a working-class family ceased as 'George had an instinctive genius for housework'
(p.161). Through this allusion to Carpenter's domestic arrangements the reader is
invited to consider the irony of the socialist community based on the perpetuation of
the unproductive role of domestic servant.

"I can't go alone," he continued, after he had smoked some minutes in silence. "You'll have to come with me, Nell. We'll let bygone be bygones, and get married."

"Oh, George," sobbed Nelly, "I ain't worth it."

"That's nonsense," said George, shaking the ashes out of his pipe. "I'll come to-morrow evening, and we'll talk over the wedding. I must get back now to light the lamps. What are you crying about?"

"I was only thinking how nice it would have been to have baby down in the country," said Nelly.

George shook his head. He gave Nelly a kiss, and told her to expect him the next evening. He went out to the kitchen, and as he shut the door he muttered, between his teeth: —

"I wish I'd never left the Service."

Original advert from the Author's Co-operative edition.

APPENDIX A

ENGELS-HARKNESS CORRESPONDENCE

Engels's Letter to Harkness[1]

London,
Early April 1888

Dear Miss H[arkness],

I thank you very much for sending me through Messrs. Vizetelly your *City Girl*. I have read it with the greatest pleasure and avidity. It is indeed, as my friend Eichhoff your translator calls it, *ein kleines Kunstwerk*;[2] to which he adds, what will be satisfactory to you, that consequently his translation must be all but literal, as any omission or attempted manipulation could only destroy part of the original's value.

What strikes me most in your tale besides its realistic truth is that it exhibits the courage of the true artist. Not only in the way you treat the Salvation Army, in the teeth of supercilious respectability, which respectability will perhaps learn from your tale, for the first time, *why* the Salvation Army has such a hold on the popular masses. But chiefly in the plain unvarnished manner in which you make the old, old story, the proletarian girl seduced by a middle-class man, the pivot of the whole book. Mediocrity would have felt bound to hide the, to it, commonplace character of the plot under heaps of artificial complications and adornments, and yet would not have got rid of the fate of being found out. You felt you could afford to tell an old story, because you could make it a new one by simply telling it truly.

Your Mr. Arthur Grant is a masterpiece.

If I have anything to criticize, it would be that perhaps, after all, the tale is not quite realistic enough. Realism, to my mind, implies, besides truth of detail, the truthful reproduction of typical characters under typical circumstances. Now your characters are typical enough, as far as they go; but

---

1 Engels to Margaret Harkness, early 1888, *Marx and Engels on Literature and Art*, ed. Lee Baxandall and Stefan Morawski (St. Louis: Telos Press, 1973), pp.114-116. Text only; footnotes my own.
2 A small work of art.

the circumstances which surround them and make them act, are not perhaps
equally so. In "City Girl"[3] the working class figures as a passive mass, unable
to help itself and not even making any attempt at striving to help itself. All
attempts to drag it out of its torpid misery come from without, from above.
Now if this was a correct description about 1800 or 1810, in the days of
Saint-Simon and Robert Owen, it cannot appear so in 1887 to a man who
for nearly fifty years has had the honour of sharing in most of the fights of the
militant proletariat. The rebellious reaction of the working class against the
oppressive medium which surrounds them, their attempts – convulsive, half
conscious or conscious – at recovering their status as human beings, belong
to history and must therefore lay claim to a place in the domain of realism.

I am far from finding fault with your not having written a point-blank
socialist novel, a '*Tendenzroman*',[4] as we Germans call it, to glorify the social
and political views of the authors. This is not at all what I mean. The more
the opinions of the author remain hidden, the better for the work of art. The
realism I allude to may crop out even in spite of the author's opinions. Let me
refer to an example. Balzac, whom I consider a far greater master of realism
than all the Zolas *passés, présents et a venir*,[5] in *La Comédie humaine* gives us a
most wonderfully realistic history of French "Society," describing, chronicle-
fashion, almost year by year from 1816 to 1848 the progressive inroads of the
rising bourgeoisie upon the society of nobles, that reconstituted itself after
1815 and that set up again, as far as it could, the standard of *la viellie politesse
française*.[6] He describes how the last remnants of this, to him, model society
gradually succumbed before the intrusion of the vulgar moneyed upstart, or
were corrupted by him; how the grand dame whose conjugal infidelities were
but a mode of asserting herself in perfect accordance with the way she had
been disposed of in marriage, gave way to the bourgeoisie, who corned[7] her
husband for cash or cashmere; and around this central picture he groups a
complete history of French Society from which, even in economic details (for
instance the rearrangement of real and personal property after the Revolution),
I have learned more than from all the professed historians, economists, and
statisticians of the period together. Well, Balzac was politically a Legitimist;
his great work is a constant elegy on the inevitable decay of good society, his
sympathies are all with the class doomed to extinction. But for all that his

---

3   Inconsistent format in original.
4   A novel of purpose.
5   Past, present and future.
6   A respectable old French spinster.
7   *OED*, formed into grains or particles; granulated. The bourgeois woman wears
down her husband in order to get her material desires.

satyre is never keener, his irony never bitterer, than when he sets in motion the very men and women with whom he sympathizes most deeply – the nobles. And the only men of whom he always speaks with undisguised admiration, are his bitterest political antagonists, the republican heroes of the Cloître Saint Mérri,[8] the men, who at that time (1830-36) were indeed the representatives of the popular masses. That Balzac thus was compelled to go against his own class sympathies and political prejudices, that he *saw* the necessity of the downfall of his favourite nobles, and described them as people deserving no better fate; and that he *saw* the real men of the future where, for the time being, they alone were to be found – that I consider one of the greatest triumphs of Realism, and one of the grandest features in old Balzac.

I must own, in your defence, that nowhere in the civilized world are the working people less actively resistant, more passively submitting to fate, more *hébétés*[9] than in the East End of London. And how do I know whether you have not had very good reasons for contenting yourself, for once, with a picture of the passive side of working-class life, reserving the active side for another work?

---

8   Also Méry or Merry, the final place of resistance by the republican uprising in Paris over 5th and 6th June 1832 following the death of General Lamarque.
9   Dazed, in a stupor.

Harkness's Reply[10]

45 Gt. Russell Street
[5?] April 1888

Dear Mr. Engels

Thank you very much for your letter; and for your book. The book I have read already, and I shall read it again now with even greater interest than before.

I have always had a great admiration and respect for you; and I never thought that I should be thought worthy of a letter from one like yourself, who is helping to make the history of the world.

Perhaps when Eleanor comes back, you will allow me to come to see you. Many things you say about my little book are very true, especially about the want of realism in it.

It would take too long to explain in a letter my difficulties in this direction. They arise chiefly from want of confidence in my powers, I think; and also from my sex. Please accept my very grateful thanks for your kindness,

Yours very truly

Margaret E. Harkness

---

10 Enormous thanks to Terry Elkiss who kindly supplied a copy of this letter, which can be found at L 2161, Margaret E. Harkness to Friedrich Engels, 5 [?] April 1888, Marx-Engels Papers, International Institute of Social History (IISH), Amsterdam. The letter is reprinted with the kind permission of the IISH.

APPENDIX B

INVESTIGATIVE JOURNALISM

Margaret E. Harkness, 'Girl Labour in the City'
Justice, 3 March 1888, pp.4-5

I have, for the last six months, been attempting to find out something about the hours and wages of girls who work at various trades in the City. Had I known how difficult the task would be I should probably never have attempted it. Last time I heard of Mr. Besant he was sitting in his office, overwhelmed with figures and facts. He said then that he did not expect to publish anything about the work of girls and women in the United Kingdom under a year or eighteen months. I do not wonder at it. Apart from the method of his enquiry, I know how exceedingly difficult it is to arrive at the truth; the tact and patience it needs to make such investigations. Employees and employers take very different views of the same circumstances; one must listen to both and then split the difference.

There are at the present time absolutely no figures to go upon if one wishes to learn something about the hours and wages of girls who follow certain occupations in the City. The factory inspectors (admirable men, but very much overworked) come, with the most naïve delight, to visit any person who has information to give about the people over whose interests they are supposed to watch with fatherly interest. Clergymen shake their heads, or refer one to homes and charities. One has to find out the truth for oneself. Both employers and employees must be visited. Even then one must wait days and weeks to inspire them with confidence, for thus alone can one obtain a thorough knowledge of things as they really are, and arrive at facts unbiassed (*sic*) by prejudice.

So far I have found that there are, at least, 200 trades at which girls work in the City. Some employ hundreds of hands, and some only fifty or sixty. Printers give the greatest amount of work, perhaps, but there are at least 200 other occupations in which girls earn a living, namely, brush makers, button makers, cigarette makers, electric light fitters, fur workers, Indiarubber stamp machinists, magic lantern slide makers, perfumers, portmanteau makers, spectacle makers, surgical instrument makers, tie makers, &c., &c. These girls can be roughly divided into two classes: those who earn from 8s. to 14s., and those who earn from 4s. to 8s. per week. Taking slack time into consideration it is, I think, safe to say that 10s. is the average weekly wage of the first class and 4s. 6d. that of the second class. Their weekly wage often falls below this, and sometimes rises above it. The hours are almost invariably from 8 a.m. to 7 p.m., with one hour for dinner and a half-holiday on Saturday. I know few cases in which such girls work less; a good many in which overtime reaches to ten or eleven at night; a few in which overtime means all night. There is little to choose between the two classes. The second are allowed by their employers to wear old clothes and boots, the first must make "a genteel appearance."

I often hear rich women say, "Oh, working girls cannot be very poor; they wear such smart feathers." If these women knew how the girls have to stint in underclothing and food in order to make what their employers call "a genteel appearance," I think they would pass quite another verdict. I will give two typical cases: A girl living just over Blackfriars Bridge, in one small room, for which she pays 5s., earns 10s. a week in a printer's business. She works from 8 a.m. to 6 p.m., then returns home to do all the washing, cleaning, cooking &c., that is necessary in a one-room establishment. She has an invalid mother dependent on her efforts, and is out-patient herself at one of the London hospitals. She was sixteen last Christmas. Another girl, who lives in two cellars near Lisson Grove, with father, mother, and six brothers and sisters, earns 3. 6d. a week in a well known factory. She is seventeen years old, but does not look more than ten or eleven. Every morning she walks a mile to her work, arriving at eight o'clock; every evening she walks a mile back, reaching home about seven o'clock. If she arrives at the factory five minutes late she is fined 7d. If she stays away a whole day she is "drilled," that is, kept without work a whole week. Her father has been out of employment for six months, so her weekly 3s. 6d. goes into the family purse. Her food consists of three slices of bread and butter, which she takes to the factory for dinner; one slice of bread and butter and some weak tea for supper and breakfast. These cases are not picked. They are to be found scattered all over London. Many and many a family is at the present time being kept by the labour of one or two such girls, who can at the most earn a few shillings. When one thinks what the life of a young girl is in happy families, all the joyousness of which she is capable, until sorrow sets its seal on her, one's heart aches for the sad lives of these girls in the City.

"And still her voice comes ringing
    Across the soft still air,
And still I hear her singing,
    'O, life, though art most fair!'"[1]

A young girl is capable of feeling in one brief hour more intense delight than a boy of her age experiences in a fortnight. Yet all this joyousness is ruthlessly stamped upon by competition, and thousands of girls in London have no enjoyment except to gaze at monstrosities in penny gaffs, or to dance on dirty pavements; and generally these poor things are too tired even to do that. It is strange that the public take so little interest in these girls considering they must become mothers of future citizens. "The youth of a nation are the trustees of posterity."[2] What sort of daughters are these girls with their pinched faces and stunted bodies likely to give England? What will posterity say of the girl labour that now goes on in the City? I have seen strong men weeping because they have no bread to give their children; I know at the London docks chains have been replaced by wooden barriers, because starving men behind pressed so hard on starving men in front, that the latter were nearly cut in two by the iron railings; I have watched a contractor mauled when he had no work to give, and have myself been nearly killed by a brick-bat that was hurled at a contractor's head by a man whose family was starving; but I deliberately say of all the victims of our present competitive system I pity these girls the most. They are so fragile. Honest work is made for them almost impossible, and if they slip, no one gives them a second chance. They are kicked and spat upon by the public. I know that the girl-labour question is but a portion of the larger labour question, that nothing can be done for them at present; but I wish that they were not the victims of the laissez-faire policy in two ways instead of one; I wish that their richer sisters were not so terribly apathetic about them.

---

1   An unknown poem or song.

2   The final line of Benjamin Disraeli's *Sybil* (1845) as the narrator looks to the future with hope: 'That we may live to see England once more possess a free Monarchy and a privileged and prosperous People, is my prayer: that these great consequences can only be brought about by the energy and devotion of our Youth is my persuasion. We live in an age when to by young and to be indifferent can be no longer synonymous. We must prepare for the coming hour. The claims of the Future are represented by suffering millions; and the Youth of a Nation are the trustees of Posterity.'

Margaret E. Harkness, 'Home Industries'
Justice, 28 August 1888, p.2

While we congratulate the match-box girls on their strike, and say they have done well to show the public mind as such that "the little ones must stand in the thickest of the fight,"[3] we ought not to forget the poor home-workers who have been thrown out of employment by the action of these plucky young women. The match-box girls realise this, and on the 14th ult. after they had received their wages in Mr. Charrington's Hall[4] on Mile End Waste, not a few wanted to make a collection for the "ins-and-outs" workers, i.e., the makers of the trays and covers of match-boxes. The most natural thing to be done in times of tribulation is to "make a collection." We all remember the three shipwrecked mariners who sent round a hat because not one of them could remember a prayer! And yet they felt that they must pacify the angry elements by a religious ceremony.

It will be impossible to get enough money for the "ins-and-outs" workers if we made a dozen collections; nor could the London Trade Unionists, I believe, help them to any great extent, for the work comes to these unfortunate people through middlemen, and not direct from the factory. And whole families depend on the 2¼d. per gross work of the match-box makers, who are so poor that often they cannot carry the work back to the middleman because they have no string or thread to tie the boxes up with.

I have during the last three months seen a variety of home-industries, and certainly some of the worst cases have been the women who make match-boxes, or powder-boxes. The latter are paid at 1d. per gross. But other home work is almost as badly paid, and every day the pay gets less in the line of "home business;" for many men who are out of work now take to these small occupations, and the wives of clerks and tradesmen, who are being crushed beneath the wheels of the Juggernaut of competition, now undersell the women who a few years ago controlled the whole of the home-industry market.

---

3   The final two lines of the first stanza of 'Life and Death' (1861) by Adelaide Anne Procter (1825-1864), daughter of Bryan Waller Procter (1787-1874) who published poetry under the pseudonym Barry Cornwall.

4   *Mr. Charrington's Hall*: Frederick Charrington (1850-1936), heir to the Charrington brewing fortune, renounced the production of alcohol after witnessing a drunken man beat his wife and turned to social reform. The hall mentioned was part of the Tower Hamlets Mission at 31 Mile End Road, which seated five thousand people.

The women who ply the most disagreeable home-industry are, I think, the fur-pullers. As yet this work cannot be done by machinery, and the workers receive 1s. 1d. per five dozen rabbit skins. Anyone who has visited the homes of these fur-pullers must feel the words of those who congratulate themselves on cheap fur cloaks or fur hats a cruel mockery. The fur-puller sits in a barn, scraping the skins of rabbits, with the fluff in her hair, nose and mouth, choked and half-blinded. I hear that the Brompton Hospital for Consumption is the home of these women when they are "past working." Canvas workers who make break covers, blinds for shops, tents, coal sacks, etc., may be seen in the East End, staggering home with heavy loads on their heads or their hips, which in course of years makes their bodies bent or crooked. The pay is 2s. for twelve sacks, 5s. 6d. for ten hammocks, etc. One woman near Aldgate, who makes sacks for the Navy, receives 4s. for ten large sacks, each of which has eight holes in it; four splices, and two patches; each of which must be sewn, roped, and marked with a broad arrow for Government. She works from 5a.m. to 8 p.m., standing; and some idea of what canvas work is like can be had from the fact that she has sprained both her wrists over it.

Brush-making is another large home industry, and so badly paid that the workers say it is hardly worth while to fetch the work and carry it back again. The pay for filling in one hundred holes, and fastening the fibre or hair with wire, is generally a penny, sometimes a half-penny per brush.

I have seen girls and women, who are employed by umbrella manufacturers, knitting tops of tassels at 4s. 6d. per gross, and it is such fine work that one gross takes them a week; fastening button, ring and flap to elastic bands for the umbrellas at 4d. per gross; making neckties at 1s. 9d. per gross; bows for boys at 10d. per gross; button holes for 2¼d. per gross, and so on ad infinitum. I have not spoken here of the many small industries which women do on their own account. I have mentioned a few of the industries which are given to them by factories or shops at a starvation rate of payment. Weaving is dying out as a home employment, but I have visited a woman who made the binding for the Queen's Jubilee carriages. She received 2½d. per yard for it; and produced six yards a day by sitting at her loom from morning till evening. The "Star"[5] speaks of this woman and says one day it will have the devil's own tale to tell of home industries. I doubt very much if the "Star" will ever do it, but I am sure if the public knew what the hours of work are for these unfortunate women, and their pay, people would shudder to think of the price in blood and flesh that is paid by the workers in order that the rich

---

5   A London evening newspaper founded by T. P. O'Connor in 1888 and which ceased publication in 1960.

may congratulate themselves on bargains. There is no doubt that the public conscience is beginning to wake up on this subject, for the capitalist press is talking about home industries, and they will have a place in the forthcoming Blue-book on female labour, [6] and at Mr. Besant's conference in October. But will people agree to the economic changes which must be made before any real help can be given to those who are engaged in home industries? Feeling that something must be done, they will, I think, try to make a collection. Readers of JUSTICE may be interested to hear that several people are now engaged in making a collection of another sort, namely a museum of home industries. When this is exhibited the public will see the articles ticketed with two prices, first that at which they are sold, secondly that at which they are given out to the home workers by the manufacturers and shops.

---

6   In 1888 Beatrice Potter (later Webb) testified at the Lord's Select Committee on the Sweating System which was subsequently published by Hansard as *Report[s] from the Select committee of the House of lords on the sweating system, vol. 1* (1888).

APPENDIX C

SHORT FICTION

John Law, 'Little Tim's Christmas'
Pall Mall Gazette, 24 December 1890, pp.1-2

The sun lay like a red ball in the foggy sky, high up above the London houses. One could not see across the street, or recognize the faces of passers-by, for the yellow fog blinded one's eyes and confused ones senses. It was thick in the City thickest of all in the Borough.[1]

There, in a garret, two little boys stood with their faces pressed to a pane of glass, watching the red ball and wondering.

"What is it, Tim?" asked the youngest.

"Er's the moon, Bill," replied Tim. "When I was down 'opping[2] I seed 'er all bloody like that, and Sally said 'er was the 'Arvest moon. I guess 'er's come to Lunnon."

A knock on the door made the children draw their faces quickly away from the window.

"'Ush!" whispered Tim to his brother, "I guess it's School Board[3] after us."

The knock came again. Tim went softly to the door, and peeped through the keyhole.

"It's Sally!" he cried; "I'll unlock the door."

"I thought you was School Board," he explained, as an old woman came into the room carrying a jug. "Mother's took our boots, and 'er said if School Board comed we wosn't to let 'im in. What 'ave you got in that jug?"

"Wos mother drunk?" inquired the visitor, without heeding his question.

---

1   An area of London, south of the Thames, between Southwark and Newington. It was a poverty-stricken area in the nineteenth century.

2   Picking hops in Sussex and Kent during the hop harvest. Many of the poorest London inhabitants would travel to the hop farms to earn money during the harvest. In Southwark, a Hop Exchange was opened in 1866.

3   State controlled schools founded after the 1870 Education Act to ensure an education for all children were run by elected boards were funded through the rates. The boards would not personally trace absent children but would employ school inspectors to check on truancy.

"Well, 'er slept 'eavy last night."

"'Ave yer had any breakfast?"

"Nothink. Baby's cried 'isself to sleep, and Bill and me's been lookin' at the 'arvest moon, what you and me seed when we wos 'opping. What's in the jug?"

"Tea."

"Tea!"

"Yes, my son. Taste it." Sally poured something out of the jug into two broken teacups, and handed it to the children.

"Good?" she asked.

"Prime!" said Tim.

"Sweet?"

"Treacle!"

Sally chuckled. She was old and weather-beaten; dressed in rags and a crape bonnet. Wrinkles scored her face, creases furrowed her neck; her eyes were sunk deep down in their sockets, but they smiled lovingly on the boys while she watched them enjoying her own scanty breakfast.

"'Ere's summat for the fire," she said, opening her apron, which she held together with a horny hand, and showing Tim some bits of paper and a few cinders. "Got any sticks?"

Tim pointed to a broken box on the hearth.

She set to work.

"Now I'll be off," she said, when a fire burnt in the grate. "If anyone comes after me, just yer say 'Does yer want rags sorted?' and if the party says 'Yes,' then yer say, 'Well, Sally wun't be 'ome for a bit.'"

"All right," said Tim. "When will you be back?"

"Not before one, sonny."

Saying this, the old woman left the room, casting a glance at the fire that gleamed through the fog, and a hasty look at the red ball in the sky which Tim called the "'arvest moon." She knew it was the sun, but why should she confuse the minds of the children?

After the door was shut the boys went to the fire and crouched down on the hearth. Yellow fog filled the room, hiding the old bed where the baby lay under dirty blanket, and throwing a curtain over the broken chairs and boxes. Tim held his hands up before the burning sticks. He looked wondrous wise in the firelight. Gleams fell on his small white face, showing his wizened features, from which all traces of childhood seemed to have vanished. He had been the sole protector of his two little brothers for the space of a year and a half, ever since his father found a home in the cemetery. His mother drank, and when drunk she was sometimes violent. He had seen a good deal of life, although he was only eight, for he lived in a Southwark[4] lodging-house. Fights, murders, suicides, and deaths made epochs in his existence and he talked of "when I wos young" as though the time lay far back in his memory.

Presently the baby began to cry, and Tim went to fetch it from the bed. He brought it to the fire, and fed it with some of the tea which old Sally had given to him for his breakfast. While he was busy with the baby, Bill crawled to the window.

"Oh, Tim!" he said, "the red ball 'as gone out o' the sky."

"I guess," said Tim, "'er's gone back to the country."

Then Tim's thoughts wandered to the days when he had gone hopping with old Sally, to the harvest moon and the hop-fields. He would have been perfectly happy then if he had not "worried" about the children.

"When I wos young," he said aloud, "I never worried about nothink."

Just as the words were said a shrill cry came fro the window.

"What's the matter?" asked Tim.

"I's cut me thumb wid a bit o' glass," sobbed Bill.

"Come to the light and let me see," said Tim.

The little boy came howling to the hearth, holding out his thumb, and pointing to the blood upon it.

"Whatever will I do?" exclaimed Tim. "It's lock-jaw[5] he's got; I knows it."

Only the week before a man had died from lock-jaw in the room below the garret; and Tim had heard his mother discussing the matter with her neighbours. "If they'd stuck his jaws open directly he cut his thumb, he'd a pulled through," some one had said, "but all the doctors in London couldn't force his jaws open after he got to the hospital."

Tim laid the baby on the bed, where it lay crying as loud as it could cry, because it was cold and famished; then he went back to the fireplace, and found a square piece of stick.

"Old yer moth open," he said to Bill.

The little boy stopped crying and opened his mouth.

Tim slipped the stick between his teeth. "Now," said Tim, "come along to the 'ospital."[6]

But Bill threw himself on the floor and kicked. His thumb was bleeding,

---

4   Lodging houses were usually for temporary accommodation, which would be paid for by the night. Tim's life spent in the lodging house signifies the grinding poverty he was born into.

5   The symptoms of the bacterial infection tetanus include muscular spasms which usually begin in the jaw.

6   Probably Guy's Hospital in Southwark, founded in 1721 by Thomas Guy.

and he felt suffocated, so he rolled on the ground until he lost his breath. Directly he became pale and still, Tim picked him up and struggled with him out of the room and down the staircase. No one saw the children leave the house for the place was full of fog and very dark; so they arrived in the street, where Tim laid his brother down on the pavement, and stopped to pant and stretch his arms for a minute. Then he picked Bill up again, and struggled bravely along with his burden until he reached the hospital.

"What is it?" inquired the hospital porter as he passed through the gate.

"Lock-jaw, sir!" panted Tim.

"I thought it was a bundle of rags," said the man; "there, to the left, that's the Out-patient's Department."

Tim struggled into the receiving-room, holding his brother tightly round the waist.

"What is it?" asked a doctor.

"Lock-jaw," gasped Tim, "but I've stuck his jaws open."

Loud peals of laughter made him stare at the doctors and students who had gathered round Bill.

"Ain't it lock-jaw?" he whispered to a nurse, who was standing by.

"No," said the woman, "of course it isn't."

For a moment Tim could not believe his senses. Then an awful vision floated before him, a vision of his mother. Supposing she came home while he was away, and found the baby alone, crying? What would happen then? It is but a step, they say, from the sublime to the ridiculous; but sometimes that step is across a precipice. Tim shuddered when he heard the students laughing at his mistake. He had meant to save Bill's life, and all he had done was to make himself a laughing-stock.

Without a word he took his brother hand and left the hospital. Bill trotted by his side through the foggy street, pointing to the sticking-plaster on his thumb, and chattering about the penny he had received from one of the medical students.

"P'raps mother ain't come home," thought Tim, "or p'raps 'er's so drunk 'er wun't see us!"

Part II

An hour later the doors of the hospital receiving-room were pushed open by old Sally, the rag sorter. She hurried through them, carrying little Tim, whose head lay against her ragged dress, while his arms and legs dangled down, and blood streamed from his forehead.

"Why, this is the boy who came here an hour ago with the lock-jaw case," said the doctor, when Sally laid Tim on the table.

The students crowded round to look, but they did not laugh at Tim now, for they thought he was dead. They listened to the doctor's questions, and watched old Sally's face while she explained that the boy had fallen on the hearth in the garret.

"Is he your grandson?" inquired the doctor while he felt Tim's pulse.

"No, he ain't. I'm a lone woman. I've got no children. I fend for myself."

"Well, it's a matter for the police," the doctor said. "I believe the boy has been knocked down, or kicked; his head's smashed."

The fog had lifted by the time Sally left the hospital. She went back to the lodging-house, up the staircase, and into her room. Rags covered the floor. A large heap of rags made a bed, another heap served as a seat. A horrid stench filled the place, but Sally was accustomed to the smell, and she never opened the window, saying that she liked to be "warm and comfortable." While she was raking the cinders together in the grate, and patting a black cat that had raised its back to welcome its mistress, the door was opened, and Tim's mother came in with the baby in her arms, and Bill hanging to her skirt.

"Sally," she said, "I was drunk when I did it!"

"Yes, yer wos," said Sally, "and yer'd best make yerself scarce, for the pleece 'as been told, and if yer don't take yerself off yer'll swing for it."

"Will he die?"

"The doctor says 'e ull."

"Will you mind the children a bit?"

"Yes, till Christmas."

The woman placed the baby on the heap of rags and vanished.

Each day Sally visited the hospital, and sat beside the bed on which Tim lay unconscious. Tears streamed down her cheeks, and she wiped them away with the back of her hand, saying to the nurse, "I've loved 'im like a son. I'm a lone woman. I never had no children."

At last, on Christmas Eve, when she went to the hospital at about seven o'clock, she found Tim himself again.

She sat down beside him, smoothing out her ragged dress, and trying to make her crape bonnet sit straight upon her head. Tim's white face frightened her, and she could not speak. She did not want him to see that she was crying.

A great fire blazed opposite Tim's bed, and round the fire sat boys and men, reading, playing games, and discussing politics. Nurses flitted about, decorating the walls with ivy and holly, while they chatted to one another and laughed with the patients. No one seemed to be very ill except Tim, but a single glance at his face told Sally he was dying.

"Tim, my son," she said at last, "this is a beautiful place, ain't it?"

"Yes," answered Tim faintly, "it's like 'eaven."

Neither spoke again for a few minutes. Then Tim pointed to some toys on the bed.

"Take 'em 'ome to the children," he said. "When I wos young I set my 'eart on a top like this un 'ere what I've got for Christmas. Take it 'ome to Bill."

The old woman pretended to admire the toys, while her tears dropped on the blanket.

"Sally," said Tim presently, "does you remember when we went 'opping?"

"Yes, my son."

"Well, that wos like this 'ere 'ospital; it wos like 'eaven."

Old Sally's eyes wandered over the ward, and she admired the decorations. Tim lay with his eyes shut, thinking of the time when he had gone hopping. He had "worrited" then about the children, and now he felt that he was going away from them for a long time, going to the strange land his father had talked about when he "wos young." He was not sorry to go but he could not help "worriting" about the children. One of the nurses began to sing a Christmas carol, and Tim opened his eyes to look at her. Then he saw old Sally beside his bed, dressed in the same ragged dress, and the same old crape bonnet she had worn when they went into the country together. Sally had always been good to him and he knew that she never broke a promise.

"Sally," he said, "when I'm gone yer'll look after the children?"

"Yes, my son," said Sally, "I ull."

Tim gave a sigh of relief. He closed his eyes again, and by the time the nurse had finished singing he was asleep, with one hand under his cheek and the other in Sally's horny fingers.

The next morning when the sun was shining, and the Christmas bells were ringing, Sally went again to the hospital. A heavy snow had fallen during the night, and now the Borough was covered with a white pall that hid all its deformities. Children shouted while they snow-balled passers-by, and the policemen pretended not to see what was going on, unless (by some accident) a snowball hit them. Everyone seemed to rejoice because King Sol[7] had put in an appearance, for he comes seldom to London, so he gets a right royal welcome.

"Don't go upstairs," said the porter after Sally had climbed the hospital

---

7   The sun. Presumably the closure of the local factories for Christmas day has meant that the air has been cleared of some of the pollutants that cause smog.

steps, "your little lad's not there any longer."

"Where may 'e be?"

"I'll show you."

She followed the porter along the passages and down a staircase.

"Is 'e dead?" she asked, when the porter stopped to unlock a door.

"Yes, I've just brought him down here," said the porter.

Old Sally went into the mortuary, and stood crying while the man uncovered a little coffin. There lay Tim, with a smile on his face, and his hands holding a bit of holly, "because it was Christmas."

For a minute Sally looked silently at him. Then she bent down to kiss his forehead. "Tim, my son," she whispered, "I wun't forget my promise."

It is several years since little Tim went home to the cemetery. His mother has not been heard of since. The children live in Sally's room, with the cat. Bill has developed a genius for sorting rags, and the baby has been taught to pick out the papers from the rubbish Sally finds in the dust heaps.

Somehow or other the old woman manages to pay the rent and to provide food for the children; how she does this is only known to herself. She has not forgotten little Tim. Often at dusk, before she lights the dip candle, she calls the boys to the fire, and says:

"Now, my sons, I ull just tell yer 'ow yer brother Tim kept 'is last Christmas!"

Victorian Secrets

Victorian Secrets is an independent publisher dedicated to producing high-quality books from and about the nineteenth century, including critical editions of neglected novels.

All Sorts and Conditions of Men by Walter Besant

The Angel of the Revolution by George Chetwynd Griffith

The Autobiography of Christopher Kirkland by Eliza Lynn Linton

The Beth Book by Sarah Grand

The Blood of the Vampire by Florence Marryat

The Dead Man's Message by Florence Marryat

Demos by George Gissing

East of Suez by Alice Perrin

Henry Dunbar by Mary Elizabeth Braddon

Her Father's Name by Florence Marryat

The Light that Failed by Rudyard Kipling

A Mummer's Wife by George Moore

Not Wisely, but Too Well by Rhoda Broughton

Robert Elsmere by Mrs Humphry Ward

Selected Stories of Morley Roberts

Sowing the Wind by Eliza Lynn Linton

Thyrza by George Gissing

Twilight Stories by Rhoda Broughton

Vice Versâ by F. Anstey

Weeds by Jerome K. Jerome

Weird Stories by Charlotte Riddell

Workers in the Dawn by George Gissing

For more information on any of our titles, please visit:

www.victoriansecrets.co.uk